The Trip

By Robin Alexander

THE TRIP
© 2015 BY ROBIN ALEXANDER

ISBN 13: 978-1-935216-75-9

First Printing: 2015

This Trade Paperback Is Published By
Intaglio Publications
Walker, LA USA
WWW.INTAGLIOPUB.COM

CREDITS

EXECUTIVE EDITOR: TARA YOUNG
COVER DESIGN BY: Tiger Graphics

Dedication

For all of those wonderful people who write to me and fluff up my ego with their kind words of praise.

Acknowledgments

As always, I want to give a shout-out to Tara and my editorial team. I love y'all BIG.

Chapter 1

"If you get up, you're gonna die. We're supposed to stay seated any time the Winnebago is moving," Ella Savoy said as she shuffled a deck of cards.

"Stuff it, Ella. I'm thirsty. What's the use of traveling in one of these things if we can't stretch our stems every now and then? You want some tea?"

Ella gave Anne Jacoby a stern look over the top of her glasses. "I want you to sit down."

"Well, I ain't. Where'd you hide those peanut butter cookies?"

"Jill, Anne is up walking around," Ella yelled loudly.

Jill glanced into the rearview mirror that enabled her to see what was going on in the camper behind her. "Have you two regressed to childhood?" she ground out. "Anne, sit down, and, Grandma, quit tattling every five minutes. We've only been on the road for two hours, and y'all are already driving me crazy."

"Anne is still up."

"Shut up, Ella! Where's the cookies?"

"Grandma," Jill said between clenched teeth. "Tell her where the damn cookies are so she will sit down."

"Don't you cuss my sister," Anne shouted. "We may be old, but the two of us together will beat your ass."

Jill responded by turning up the radio.

Ella chuckled. "We couldn't beat a gnat's ass. The cookies are in the pantry, dingbat."

1

Anne grabbed a container of tea from the fridge and the pack of cookies. She returned to the table and sat with a grunt. "When're we stopping for lunch?"

"It's eight o'clock in the morning, so I expect we'll eat around noon." Ella lowered her voice. "Do you think Shay is sleeping?"

"We'd be able to know for sure if you didn't squawk every time I got up," Anne said as she opened the cookies. "They don't seem very interested in each other."

"Well, they just met. They'll have plenty of time on this trip to get to know each other and become cozy."

Anne stuffed a cookie in her mouth and tried to speak around it. "This is harebwained."

"Shay is a pretty little thing, a lesbian, single, and she's very sweet. I'm not trying to play matchmaker. I see this as a chance for Jill to get to know someone with substance. At home, she's too busy chasing…well…" Ella sighed. "Trash. There, I said it."

"So you're gonna mash them together and hope they blend, sounds like a recipe for disaster. Jill's gonna see right through this scheme. She probably already has, and I guarantee you, she's gonna rebel. She can be a downright shit when she wants to be. Sleeping booty back there in the bedroom might slap her teeth out. Instead of the harmonious match you hope to make, you may end up with something that will make the Hatfields and McCoys pale in comparison."

"Have a little faith," Ella said as she snagged a cookie. "There's no scheme. This is just a chance for Jill to get to know someone outside of her usual."

"You keep saying that, but I don't believe it, and Jill won't, either. Shay's gonna figure out that you and Chloe led her to the slaughter, and she's gonna be pissed, too." Anne waved a cookie. "Here's something else to consider. Shay is Chloe's favorite niece, she's biased. Shay had been living in Utah for years, then all of the sudden, she packed up and came here with no job prospects. That tells me she was running from something or someone. Maybe it's the mob, or she could've done something illegal. You don't really know her, and Chloe's adoration keeps her from looking for the truth."

"The mob, really?" Ella shook her head. "Chloe knows exactly what happened, and she told us. Shay was in a relationship that wasn't going anywhere, so she ended it. She was born and raised in Baton Rouge, and she simply came home to make a fresh start." Ella smacked her lips. "I have done my part, and now we will sit back and let lesbian nature run its course."

"I like lesbians. They wear sensible clothes, and they're good with their hands. I mean that strictly in a carpentry and mechanical sense."

"That's so stereotypical." Ella shuffled the deck of cards. "There are all kinds of lesbians. Haven't you learned anything from Jill?"

"Yeah, she ain't handy when it comes to us. That cabinet door she fixed the other day fell right off. I've given up all hope of having her build us a doghouse."

Ella leaned close to the table and met Anne's gaze. "We don't have a dog. How many times do I have to tell you that?"

"But a doghouse gives the illusion of one." Anne tapped her temple with her finger. "If people believe we have one, they'll think twice about coming in our yard."

"You have got to slack off on those pills you take to make you sleep." Ella sat up straight when the camper slowed. "Are we stopping?"

"Restroom break," Jill said. "You two stay seated until I get this thing into a parking space. Then you can raid the pantry."

Jill found a spot, parked, then tore out the door like she was on fire. She walked past the restrooms to the walking trails beyond. They'd just begun the trip, and already, she needed space. Anne and Ella were being cantankerous, that was nothing new, but with every mile, angry tension built up and seemed to rest on Jill's neck like a boulder. She'd been living under the delusion that something would arise and the plans would be canceled, but when her ass hit the seat of the Winnebago that morning, reality smacked her hard.

"I'm gonna punch Anne in the forehead and duct tape her ass to a seat. Grandma is gonna get a taping, too, right in the mouth. If I had any girl balls, I'd park that rolling bitch at the

3

first campground after the Florida state line and say, 'Here we are, folks, suck it up and enjoy it while you can because we're going home tomorrow.'"

Jill could grouse all she wanted in private, but she would never say anything like that to Ella. She dearly loved her grandmother and Anne, who technically wasn't her great-aunt by blood. Anne had been Ella's best friend even before Jill's father was born and was a part of the family.

The Savoy family was close-knit. Just about all of them worked in the family steel business, except for Jill's youngest brother, Jude, who had rebelled and gone to law school. When Ella and Anne announced that they wanted to travel up the eastern seaboard in the Winnebago, Jill's father assigned her as driver and tour guide. Jill wouldn't have normally balked at a two-week vacation, but she'd left behind a ton of work to traipse around with two old arguing women and a complete stranger.

"Inhale deeply, let it out slowly," Jill chanted softly as she walked as fast as her feet would carry her.

The perfect vacation would've been one where she actually escaped her family. She was surrounded by them twenty-four/seven, and a woman needed a break every now and then. All hopes for true relaxation and freedom were flushed straight down the toilet the moment Jill's father walked into her office a month ago.

"Girl, have I got news for you," Dale Savoy said excitedly. "You've been working hard, and I think you've earned a two-week vacation this year, all expenses paid."

Dale was so tight when it came to money, he squeaked when he walked, and Jill knew she wasn't going to like what she was about to hear. "Somehow, I know you're not about to send me to the Bahamas or Cancun."

"Oh, no, something much better," Dale said with a huge smile. "I'm entrusting you with Sally."

Jill's heart began to pound, but not with excitement and joy. Sally was the name of Dale's prized Winnebago, the latest in a long line of Sallys. It was a deluxe model and cost more than Jill paid for her house, which said a lot about Dale's priorities. Jill

4

figured he was probably wearing underwear that was so old it looked like Swiss cheese. Jill's mother routinely sewed up holes in Dale's socks because he felt it was a waste of money to buy something that no one but him was ever going to see. Sally, however, had every bell and whistle known to the camping kind.

"Dad, I don't even walk near her in the driveway. I'm not going to take her anywhere," Jill said dryly.

Then Dale dropped the bombshell. "Momma and Anne want to take a trip."

Dale could tell just about everyone on the planet no, but there was one small redheaded exception. Momma usually got what she wanted from her only son. Jill knew if Dale was willing to set the keys to Sally in her hand, there was no way in hell she was going to get out of the trip.

"Dad, this isn't the right time, you know that. We just spent a fortune on a new accounting program. They're coming to install it in three weeks. When that's done, I need to be here to make sure everything is transferred correctly."

Dale waved a hand. "Your momma and Karen can take care of that. You need a vacation."

"I do, but what you're suggesting is a shitload of driving and trying to corral two women that haven't realized they're old yet. There's no enjoyment in that. I'm gonna be stressed the entire time worrying about denting or scratching your other woman."

"Momma says she believes this is the last real vacation that she and Anne will take. She wants to have this experience with you. There's no denying that you're her favorite, and before you get too testy, think about all the places she took you when you were growing up."

It is said that mothers are the only ones who truly know how to wield the sword of guilt. Dale had just sliced through Jill like butter. "Let me think about it," she said with resignation.

"Inhale deeply, exhale slowly," Jill continued to chant as her pace slowed. She looked into the woods surrounding the rest stop and actually took a moment to ponder what it would be like to live in the wild. She saw herself disappearing into the foliage, becoming feral, fighting wild animals for food while wearing clothes made from woven muscadine vines. She weighed that vision against what awaited her in the camper. The thought of deer ticks and lack of hygiene was almost as daunting.

Chapter 2

Shay Macaluso pretended to be asleep when Ella darkened the doorway of the room in the rear of the camper and whispered her name. Shay had prayed for earthquakes, hurricanes, and even a bad transmission to cancel the trip she didn't want to make. Unfortunately for her, quakes were rare in Louisiana. It was April, hurricane season didn't begin until June, and the massive Winnebago appeared to be in tiptop shape.

What she resented most was putting her new life on hold. She desperately needed a job, so she could pack up and move out of her Aunt Chloe's house. Chloe had been gracious and asked so little of her, and Shay couldn't bring herself to refuse what Chloe thought was a real treat and a big favor.

"I wouldn't ask this of you if I didn't think it was truly important. Frankly, I think Anne and Ella are too old to go traipsing around the country in a bus. I told them I'd go, only because Jill would need help taking care of them. But what help could I really be? I'm only a few years younger than they are, and my arthritis makes my hands useless most days. You're a nurse, and those women are my very best friends. You could help take care of them and have a wonderful vacation at the same time. Do this for me, won't you?"

Ebola was a tad more frightening and sickening than traveling with three people Shay didn't know. She'd met Anne and Ella at Chloe's house, but she hadn't met Jill until that morning. As first impressions go, Jill didn't make much of a

7

splash. When introduced, Jill made very little eye contact and offered an offhanded hello. Then she handled Shay's bag roughly when she stowed it in the camper.

While Chloe, Ella, and Anne chatted, Shay made her first attempt to be friendly with Jill. "Do you feel comfortable driving this bus?" she asked with a smile.

"This is a custom-outfitted Winnebago and costs more than most of the houses on this block. She is not a bus," Jill said dismissively before she climbed in and didn't come back out before they left.

"But you are most definitely an asshole," Shay said softly. "What the hell am I doing?"

The next log on the proverbial beaver dam crushing Shay beneath its weight was the fact that Jill Savoy was one of *those* women. She was exceptionally good-looking, with just the right amount of muscle in her arms and legs that didn't make her look bulky, but rather toned and fit. Her dark jaw-length hair was still wet and looked as though she had styled it by running her fingers through it, yet it still looked perfect. Her eyes were light blue, her skin fair, she was tall and gorgeous, and it was obvious that she knew it, which made Shay despise her all the more.

Jill also had a temper, Shay realized, when she heard her yell, "You can't change the route!"

"I can and I did," Ella said defiantly. "Anne and I have decided that we don't want to go to the beaches. It's too cold for us to swim. We want to start heading north now. Lest you forget, I'm the captain of this voyage."

Anne chimed in as Shay peeked out of the bedroom at the three of them in the kitchen. "You're the monkey at the wheel. You're supposed to eat, scratch, and do what we say."

"We have reservations according to the course we were supposed to keep." Jill pinched the bridge of her nose.

"I have this magic box the kids call a cellphone." Ella grinned. "I'm going to use it to cancel the old reservations and make new ones. I won't have you driving more than eight hours a day just like we planned before."

"Dad isn't gonna like this," Jill argued. "He likes to know where his baby is at all times, and I'm not talking about me."

"He'll get over it," Ella said with a flip of her hand. "Now let's plot a course to Chattanooga."

"Tennessee?" Jill practically screamed.

Anne clapped and laughed. "Jillian knows her states, I'm so proud."

Jill shot Anne a look. "Tennessee is full of hills, some of them are steep, and I'm not used to driving Sally on that kind of terrain. Dad is gonna shit a kitten, and he isn't going to yell at you two, but he'll let me have it. The monkey at the wheel is staying the course."

"I'll take care of my son." Ella poked Jill in the chest. "You've been driving these things since you were a teen. I've seen you shoehorn campers into tiny places that most people couldn't put a car. A few hills aren't a challenge for you. Now if it'll make you feel better, we'll put it to a vote."

"You've already voted, it's two to one in your favor," Jill spat out.

"Nope, to be fair, we'll call in—"

Before the name could pass Ella's lips, Anne bellowed, "Shay!" at the top of her lungs.

Shay steeled herself and walked out of the room. "Yes?"

Anne gave her a disapproving look. "Are you sick?"

"No, I just have a headache," Shay said softly as the throbbing began in her temples.

Ella fished a bottle of pills from her purse and handed them to Shay before she said, "We're about to have a vote."

"Yes, I heard." Shay stared at the prescription medication bottle. "Do you take...Estradiol for headaches?"

"That's an old bottle. Frankly, I'm not sure what's in there, but I'm certain there's some acetaminophen mixed in." Ella put a hand on Shay's arm. "So tell us, do you want to stick to the same route or go north to see the sights in Tennessee, then on to West Virginia and camp at the base of those dark hills next to a clear stream?"

Shay glanced at Jill, who was shaking her head. Then at Anne, who had picked up a butter knife and was looking a little menacing. Shay decided that she'd rather piss off the monkey with the steering wheel than the old woman who had begun

9

running the knife across her throat. She swallowed hard and whispered, "North."

"Don't be angry."

Jill glanced at Ella, who looked like an elf in the passenger's seat. "If we had rented a camper, I'd feel much better about this. Don't you remember the time I dented the bumper of Sally number two? Dad acted like I'd shot him. It was years before he stopped whining about it."

Ella nodded. "Let me tell you what this old woman has learned. You can worry yourself half to death over nothing. Regardless of where we go, an accident can happen. Your daddy knows that. Now I want you to tell me the real reason you're so grumpy."

"I just have a lot of responsibility on my shoulders, Sally, you, Anne, and…Sheila."

"Shay," Ella corrected with a smile. "And you're full of shit. Try again, and this time, tell me the truth."

Jill tapped the steering wheel with her index finger. "I have a lot of work to do. We just switched over to a new accounting system, and I haven't had a chance to get everything up to date. Mom, who really doesn't have a clue about what she's doing, is probably thoroughly jacking it all up right now. When I go back, it'll be like completely starting over."

"Jillian," Ella began with a tone that meant a speech would surely follow. "One of the things I admire and respect about you is regardless of the fact that you work for your father, you take what you do very seriously. You put in long hours and you take care of your father's interests, unlike your brothers, who spend most of their time on a golf course. You above all deserve a real vacation, and that is precisely why I wanted you to come with us." Ella scrubbed her hands together. "Now we're on vacation, put all thoughts of work behind you and concentrate on having fun." She reached over and turned the radio up loud.

"Turn that rap shit down," Anne yelled.

Ella chuckled as she lowered the volume a bit. "Anne, we should listen to what the young poets of today have to say. We might learn something," she said and sat silent for a moment. "I

10

can only understand every other word. Booty...booty...drank...bend over...ho...breastesses."

Jill pressed a button on the steering wheel and changed the station. Ella listened for a moment and asked, "What does crunk mean?"

"I have no idea," Jill said and switched to another song.

"Put it on a big band station." Anne moved into one of the seats behind them.

Ella shook her head. "Oh, those haven't been around for years, you have to get with the times. It's all wiz on somebody and Yo-yo."

"Wiz Khalifa and Ne-Yo," Jill corrected with a laugh.

"Whatever. I'm hungry." Anne started to get up.

Jill checked the mirrors and changed lanes. "I am too. We'll stop in a minute if you'll wait."

Ella leaned over and looked into the back. "She got up anyway and is staggering around like a drunk giraffe. Anne! You're gonna die!"

"This is only lunch, would you two stop it with all the food?" Jill fussed as Anne handed her a jug of lemonade.

Shay totally agreed but didn't say anything as she gazed at all the plastic containers sitting atop a tablecloth on a picnic table at a rest stop.

Jill held out her hand as Ella prepared to exit the camper. "Don't wave that at me, I'm as spry as a teen," Ella said. "I'm seventy-eight, not ninety."

Anne refused help, as well. "I'm younger than she is. Don't worry, though, we'll tell you when we need help."

"Oh, I'm well aware," Jill said and sat down.

The older women sat on one side of the table, so Shay settled in next to Jill, who was already digging into everything. There was potato salad, chicken salad, pasta salad, fruit, sliced veggies, and an assortment of dips. The centerpiece was a platter of cookies.

"Presentation is just as important as the meal itself. Wouldn't it be sad if we were all just sitting here eating sandwiches off an old scarred wooden table?" Ella asked.

Jill filled her glass with tea. "You put in a lot of aesthetics just for lunch. Where's the bread?"

Shay smiled at Jill as she passed a plate to her and took that opportunity to make conversation. "I'm very sorry that you have to do all the driving."

"Shay, honey, don't you worry about her," Ella said with a laugh. "Even if we were all able to handle that land barge, she wouldn't be happy anywhere else but the driver's seat. There aren't many things with wheels that Jill can't operate."

"But she can't fix a damn cabinet door," Anne huffed.

"It doesn't matter how many screws I put in the hinges, it is not gonna support your weight when you lean on it. And that's exactly what you do." Jill pointed at Anne. "One day, the wood is gonna give, and you'll be on the floor."

"I open the cabinet and get out a pot, that's all I do," Anne argued.

"You use it as a crutch," Ella said and smiled when Anne shot her a look.

Anne and Ella continued to argue, and as they did, both of them added food to each other's plates. Ella made a sandwich, carefully cut it in half and slipped it onto Anne's plate. Anne spooned potato salad onto Ella's and added a small tag of grapes.

The older pair dressed similarly, at least from the waist up. Both of them wore jeans and cotton button-down shirts. Anne's was a striped pattern and Ella's pink and white checked. Shay silently mused that Anne and Ella must've used the same hairdresser as her Aunt Chloe. They were all in the tease and spray club. Ella's bright red hair looked almost like a fluffy ball atop her head, and Anne's was shaped like a hat Shay had seen Napoleon wearing in a painting. It was high and rounded on the top, swooped down and stuck out like a ledge on the sides and back of her head. Anne was nearly as tall as Jill, which Shay figured to be around five-foot-nine, and Ella was just a tiny waif who looked as though she barely hit five feet.

"You're a quiet one."

Shay suddenly realized that Anne was speaking to her, and she smiled. "I was just wondering how long you've known each other."

Anne patted Ella on the shoulder. "We met sixty-one years ago when Ella and John moved in next door to me and my husband. I was only sixteen and had just been married. I wasn't knocked up, we just got hitched young back in those days. I still remember Ella standing at the front door of that little duplex nine months pregnant, her stomach poking out like a melon," Anne said with a laugh. "She was just a fussin' at John because he wasn't being gentle with their things. The poor fella was trying to do it all by himself, so I roused Chester off the couch and told him he needed to help the new neighbors. We had dinner together that night, and Ella and I have been joined at the hip ever since. When she and John bought a house, Ches and I decided we needed to have one in the same neighborhood, so we bought one a block away."

Ella stared off into the distance with a winsome smile on her face. "We've outlived spouses and friends, seen presidents come and go, wars, storms—"

"The rise of New Coke, then its gruesome death," Anne added with a nod. "That was a disaster, let me tell you what."

"Sometimes it just seems like a flash, a whole life was just a moment in time," Ella said with a sigh and picked up her sandwich.

"So, Shay, how come you left Utah so fast? Did you rob a bank or something?" Anne asked, then glared at Ella when she punched her in the hip.

Thrown off by the unexpected question, Shay cleared her throat. "I just got homesick."

Ella nailed Anne in the hip again when she asked, "How do they treat lesbians up there?"

"I…never had any trouble," Shay said and took a big bite of her sandwich.

Anne nodded. "Things are changing down here, but a lot of people are still pinheads. They don't want queers to marry—"

"I hate that word, and you know it, Anne," Ella spat out.

13

"It's a real word, gay people use it all the time." Anne shrugged and continued. "They don't want gay people to marry, and they say it's because of their religion. I'll tell you what, church folk didn't think a thing about marrying girls just out of puberty to grown men back in the day. They have a problem now with two adults that want to pledge their lives to each other, the bunch of haughty hypocrites."

"Don't get wound up, you know what it does to your blood pressure." Ella clapped her hands together. "Oh, I can't wait to see the mountains in Tennessee and the Virginias. Of course, some say they're just hills unless they reach a certain elevation, but I think that's stupid. If you can fall off of it and die, it's a mountain. Jilly, did you bring your computer? Anne and I want to get on the Web and pick out some new places to see."

Anne grinned. "You know she hates to be called Jilly."

"Yes, I do, and yes, I did bring my laptop with the satellite card," Jill said. "Just don't burn it up looking at porn."

Anne perked up. "We can do that? I haven't see a—"

"No," Ella said firmly and stuffed an apple slice into Anne's mouth. "Let Shay have a day of peace before you shock and appall her."

When lunch was over and everything was packed in the camper, Jill pulled on Ella's arm and kept her from climbing in. She led her to the front of the Winnebago where they could talk in private.

"So the woman of few words is a lesbian, and she just happened to be able to go along with us at the last minute," Jill said and folded her arms.

"Chloe's arthritis...her cat is sick...she doesn't like tight spaces," Ella stammered.

"You swore to me that you would never try to fix me up with anyone after the Robbie Richards incident. That woman was under the impression that we were gonna move in together after the first date, and I didn't even kiss her. So what did you promise this one?"

"Nothing, absolutely nothing, we didn't even tell her you were a lesbian. When Chloe decided not to come on the trip, we all thought it would be good for Shay to join us because y'all do have things in common. She's around your age, and she's gay."

Ella threw up her hands. "Forgive me for thinking of you."

"You and Anne have been harping on me for months to find a nice woman and settle down. Now there's a lesbian in the Winnebago! I will date who I choose! I will get serious when I'm ready. Do not meddle. Besides, I'm seeing someone."

Ella was taken aback. "Why haven't you introduced her to me? I meet all the women you're dating."

"We've only been out a couple of times, but I like her."

"That's not seeing someone, that's..." Ella waved a hand. "That's two dates."

"And when I get home, I plan to see her again. I can find women, I don't need to be fixed up, so if you led that woman in the camper to believe—"

Ella and Jill nearly jumped out of their skin when Anne blew the horn. It was not a simple toot, but a solid blaring that lasted until Jill ran inside and snatched Anne's hand off the button.

Chapter 3

Ella got on the Web and made reservations at a state park just north of Birmingham, Alabama. Then she insisted that Shay join her and Anne for a game of Scrabble and snacks. They were seated around the table when Jill began to get testy with other drivers.

"Drive or get off the road, you jackass!"

Ella chuckled and gazed at Shay. "Jill likes to yell at the other drivers. Sometimes, she gets frothing mad, and Anne and I have to pretend we're coughing to cover our laughter. Isn't this Travel Scrabble game nice? The pieces don't move when she gets us up on two wheels."

Anne cocked her head to the side and watched as Shay spelled out "toxic." "Good job, and that's exactly what the air is gonna be like in here when these pigskins start to ferment in my gut."

"Dear Jesus," Ella said and put the heel of her hand to her forehead. "Show some decorum, woman."

"We have natural bodily functions. You are aware of this, that's why you brought a case of deodorizing spray. I'll tell you what, sister, if you think I'm gonna hold it all in and make myself miserable, you've got another think coming." Anne met Shay's gaze unabashedly. "Let it rip if you have to. It's nature."

"Urinating is nature, too, but you don't do it where everyone is sitting," Ella snapped. "So do your ripping in the bathroom."

"Oh, dear God, thank you," Jill cried from the driver's seat. "We're here, and now I don't have to kill y'all."

Ella patted Shay on the hand. "She means us, dear. You're safe."

Jill pulled up at the ranger's station, where she and Ella got out to check in. Anne took that opportunity to get to know Shay and make her feel more comfortable. "You committed a serious crime back in Utah, didn't you? Were you in one of those drug rings I see on TV?"

"No," Shay said with a laugh, unsure if she should be offended.

"Chloe said you just called her up out of the blue and asked if you could stay with her. That means you left without a whole lot of planning. Did you steal something?"

Shay looked at her like she was insane. "No…no, I didn't."

"I stole an egg once. Some tornadoes swept through Grosse Tete, and a group of us had made a bunch of food for people affected by the storm. We took it to a little church. I'd been busy all morning cooking, but on the drive over, I got hungry. We were getting ready to make plates, and I was left in a room alone with a tray of deviled eggs, so I snatched one. I was very ashamed of myself because that food was for people who'd lost a lot. I've never told anyone about that until now."

"Your secret is safe with me."

"Now you tell me one."

Shay thought for a moment. "I don't think I've ever outright stolen anything, unless you count pens from the offices I've worked in. I just forget and stick them in my pocket. I did put glue in my sister's shampoo one time because she was teasing me. I found a padlock in the field next to my house when I was around eight, and I locked my neighbor's mailbox with it." She shrugged. "I'm not sure why I did that. I blew up a dollhouse with a homemade cherry bomb made out of a ball of firecrackers a few years later. And I hit my ex in the head with a broken chair leg."

Anne leaned so close to Shay until their noses almost touched. "Are you psychotic?"

"Not when I'm taking my medication. Just don't back me into any corners, and you should be fine." Shay held up a finger.

17

"One other thing, no one needs to know what we just discussed. You can keep a secret, right?"

"I'm tight as a drum," Anne said as she sat back. "You ever done time?"

Shay pursed her lips and nodded. "I did a couple of years for aggravated assault."

"You're completely bullshitting me, aren't you?"

A slow smiled spread across Shay's face. "Not about all of it."

Anne was on the verge of another question when Ella burst into the camper all atwitter. "This place is nice! Tomorrow night, a square dance group is gonna perform at the pavilion."

"She bought us all tickets," Jill said drolly as she climbed in and went straight to the driver's seat. "I'm so damn happy."

The camper was set up, the canopy extended; Jill had even strung it with lights. She laid out the outdoor rug, then set up the table and chairs. Ella and Anne were inside cooking, and they had enlisted Shay's help. Jill could see her through the window cutting up vegetables.

Shay was not her type. It wasn't that Shay was unattractive; she just lacked the flair that Jill was normally drawn to. She liked women who were the complete opposite of her, those who wore makeup, were particular about their hair and clothes. Shay seemed like a casual girl in her running shorts and T-shirt, her dark brown hair in a ponytail.

Jill knew her grandmother well, and despite what she'd said, Ella was determined to stick an unwelcome hand in her love life. Shay didn't behave like a woman with romantic expectations, though, and Jill wondered if she had any idea what Ella was up to. Jill swatted at a mosquito that buzzed near her ear, and she continued to stare at Shay, wondering why she'd agreed to take a trip with a group of people she didn't know.

"Jill, fire up the grill," Anne called out, then laughed. "Did y'all hear me rap?"

"Jill, hook up the sewer, Jill, where's the water, Jill, light the grill," she mumbled as she poured charcoal into the pit and lit it. "This is some horse shit. Jill needs a damn beer."

18

"Here it is."

Jill turned and found Shay standing behind her with a bottle in her hand. "Thanks."

"Ella sent it. She said you earned it."

Jill took a drink and waved the bottle at Shay. "Take my advice and have a few of these, they'll help you sleep through the snore fest. They both do it, and it sounds like a couple of donkeys having sex. Don't be surprised if wild animals are surrounding the camper in the morning trying to figure out what creature is inside."

"I assume y'all really do care about each other, right?"

"Yes," Jill replied wearily. "Life is much happier and interesting with those two in it. We have a comfort level that makes it easy for us to tease and bicker. No one ever truly gets their feelings hurt, even though we love rough. I don't want to think about the day when they won't be around anymore."

"Jill, the grill, how does it feel?" Anne yelled and laughed. "Listen to me, I could be a Wiz something."

Jill held up a finger. "That day will be quieter." She walked over to the window and pressed her face to the screen. "Give it ten or fifteen minutes."

"Have you done this before—gone on an extended road trip with them?" Shay asked.

"We went to the Grand Canyon for a week, but then my mom and dad were with us. Mostly, Dad uses Sally for tailgating parties. During football season, he and Mom are always on the road. How about you—do you camp much?"

"Not as an adult. When I was a kid, my friends and I used to pitch a tent in the backyard, but that's about as deep woods as I got. This is a lot more civilized." Shay scrubbed her hands together. "I don't know anything about campers, but I'd like to help you with the things that need to be done. You're just gonna have to tell me what to do."

Jill spread her hand out over the top of the coals in the grill and tested the heat. "I'm used to managing all the hookups. I can do everything faster than I can tell you, but if I run into anything that requires an extra set of hands, I'll let you know."

19

An awkward silence settled between them for a moment. Jill took a couple of swallows of her beer as she stared up at the sky. She expected Shay to go back inside, but to her chagrin, Shay sat in one of the chairs.

"What kind of medical issues do they have?"

Jill found the question odd and replied, "General crankiness, gas, delusions of absolute power—"

The screen door opened, and Anne held out a dish. "Your time is up. I'm hungry, and I like my steak rare."

Shay rubbed her temple as she watched Jill take the steaks to the grill and lay them out. "So you don't have any idea what kind of medications they take?"

Jill turned and looked at her. "They're anti-pharmaceutical, they don't take anything unless they absolutely have to. The most you'll probably find on them is some fluid pills, so if you're looking for the good stuff, you're out of luck."

"What're you insinuating?" Shay asked as she bristled.

"You've been rubbing your forehead all day, and now you're asking about drugs, so I'll ask you straight up. Do you have a problem?"

Shay's jaw dropped. "I'm a nurse—"

"Are you talking about work?" Ella asked with a frown as she stepped outside. "This is vacation, leave all that behind. You know, I'm really surprised we haven't heard from Dale."

Jill narrowed her eyes at Shay for a second and said, "That call will come anytime now."

"You should tell him that a rock flew up and cracked Sally's windshield," Ella said with a mischievous glint in her eye. "We should make up something for each time he calls—nothing big, just a ding or a crack in something."

Shay silently seethed and wondered what Chloe had possibly told them about her. Anne had grilled her about why she'd left Utah, and Jill had basically accused her of being a drug addict.

Jill laughed. "I do not want to listen to him scream or cry. Besides, Mom would never forgive us for stoking him up."

Ella gazed at Sally. "He does love this bus, that's basically what she is, but it would infuriate him to hear me call his beloved Sally that."

Ella and Jill looked at each other and laughed when Jill's phone rang. She pulled it out of her pocket and answered. "Hi, Dad, we were just talking about you."

"How's my baby?"

"I'm fine and so is Grandma," Jill said with a grin, knowing exactly what he meant. Silence met her on the other end of the line. "Sally is fine too."

"Oh, good," Dale said with obvious relief. "Are y'all in Florida?"

"No, we're outside of Birmingham."

Dale went silent again, then said, "Honey, you do realize you went north instead of east."

"Yes, *your* mother has plotted a completely different course."

"What? Jillian, I was counting on y'all being where you said you would be. Are you telling me that y'all are wandering all willy-nilly?"

"Yep," Jill said with a nod.

"We went over the campgrounds and chose the best ones according to the stability of the sites, ease of access, and criminal history. Now you have nothing—nothing! You're in the dark."

"Yeah, it's pretty dark out here," Jill said as she looked around. "We could be on a precipice."

"Does Sally look like she's rolling?" Ella said loudly, then covered her mouth to muffle her laugh.

"Not funny," Dale bellowed. "Jillian, I hold you personally responsible. I don't care what Momma says, you're in charge. You'll end up at the Canadian border if you let her do as she pleases."

Ella held out her hand, and Jill gave her the phone. "Hi, dear," Ella said sweetly.

Dale's tone abruptly changed. "Hey, Momma, you having a good time?"

21

"I am. Jill is taking good care of us and Sally. Look, dear, Anne and I have changed our mind about the beaches. Sand makes me itch, and the water is still too chilly for swimming." Ella laughed and said, "God knows we have plenty of seashells already. The coal mines of West Virginia are calling me, and I'd like to see the mountains."

"Oh…okay, Momma. You know there're bears up there, right?"

"I would love to see a bear," Ella said enthusiastically. "From the safety of Sally, of course. Hopefully, Jill can get us close to one in its natural habitat."

"Hey, we ain't going anywhere near no damn bear," Anne said with her face pressed to the screen of the window.

"Momma, listen to Anne. She's right, bears are dangerous, and I know you have a lot of food with y'all, and they can smell—"

"Okay, a moose then," Ella said with an exaggerated sigh. "We'll just have to sail over to the Dakotas."

"Dak—what?" Dale sputtered. "Momma, put Jill back on the phone."

"I can't, dear, she's searching for the tire chocks. Now you don't worry about us at all. I have to go, the steaks are almost ready. Love you, bye."

Jill laughed when Ella handed the phone back to her. "Watch, in the next minute or so, I'm going to get a text about the chocks."

Sure enough, a text came in from Dale a minute later that read: *You mean to tell me that y'all are cooking and you haven't chocked the damn tires yet?*

Jill took the bull by the horns and texted her mother. *Mom, Grandma was screwing with Dad. Everything here is secure. Please give him a golf ball-sized Valium.*

To which her mother, Vivian, replied: *He's an idiot.*

Of the two beds behind the driver's compartment, Shay had the larger. Jill's was little more than a twin, and one of her feet hung off the side of it. Shay watched as Jill punched her pillow a few times, then flopped onto her back. "Are you uncomfortable

22

over there? Do you want to trade beds?" Shay whispered, weary of watching Jill flail around.

"Anne used a new seasoning on the meat, and it gave me heartburn, that's why I'm restless. I'm sorry if I'm keeping you awake. I feel like I could belch fire right now. You don't have a three-alarm fire going on inside your chest?"

"No, and I'm not a drug addict. If I'm to help you with them, I should have some idea of what they're taking. You told me y'all were close, I thought you'd be able to tell me anything I needed to know without having to ask them directly."

Jill reached up and switched the light on above her bed. She squinted at Shay and asked, "Are you telling me you're here in some sort of medical capacity?"

"Not officially," Shay said as she sat up. "Chloe asked me to take this trip because she was worried about them, and I'm a nurse."

Jill nodded. "That's why you're here."

Shay was taken aback by the way Jill was looking at her. "Am I missing something? Chloe practically pleaded with me to come along as a favor to her. She seemed very concerned about them."

Jill switched the light off, and Shay thought she heard suppressed laughter before a ruckus began in the bedroom. "Anne! Open a window! If you think I'm going to lie here in a cloud of your flatulence, think again," Ella said loudly. "I'm throwing those pigskins out tomorrow."

Jill howled with laughter.

"Stop poking me. I've got a bad hip, Ella. You can quit blaming your gas on me, you know the first hen that cackles laid the egg."

Jill continued to laugh like a fool at the argument going on in the back of the camper. Shay found it mildly amusing but not enough to guffaw like Jill was doing. And she accused me of having a drug problem, Shay thought and lay back down.

"You old...jackass. Control your sphincter and get your legs off of me," Ella said.

"That's not my leg."

"Then what the hell is it?"

23

"It's the decorative pillow I stuffed between us. I don't want you trying to spoon me."

"As if."

The bickering quieted, and Jill did, too. Shay stretched out and threw an arm over her eyes and tried to relax. Sleep was her only escape, and she welcomed it wholeheartedly. The sounds of night birds and crickets began to lull her, and she was reminded of the simple joy of camping in her backyard as a child. The memory of her carefree days back then was shattered by what sounded like a bullfrog followed by a high-pitched wheezing sound.

"Oh, wow," Shay said softly.

"No, that's what you say when you see Mount Rushmore for the first time. A disgusted 'oh, shit' is only appropriate here." Jill tossed a package of earplugs, and they landed squarely on Shay's chest. "I bought a whole case of these. I suggest you use them and put a pillow over your head."

Chapter 4

Shay awoke throughout the night. The first time was when Jill bumped her bed on the way to the bathroom. After that, she slept light, unused to having plugs in her ears. Every time she rolled over, she would awaken fully and look around. As the new day dawned, she gave up on sleeping altogether and lay there staring at a shaft of light growing larger on the ceiling.

At least the camper, or Sally as they called it, was nice. The driver's compartment had two captain's chairs that swiveled and reclined. The walls extended on either side behind them, and the sofas folded down into beds. There was a door and a cabinet with a TV in it above the small kitchen table that also folded out and became larger. The kitchen area was small, but it had plenty of amenities, including a dishwasher. There was a wall beyond it with plenty of cabinets, and behind it was a small restroom with a toilet and sink. Ella had mentioned there was also a washer and dryer, but Shay had not discovered where they were hidden. The master suite also had a wall that extended to make the room much larger, and there was a full bathroom with a nice shower.

What am I doing here? Shay mouthed without actually saying the words. She felt obligated to Chloe because her aunt was the one person she could truly depend on. When Shay needed a shoulder to lean on, Chloe was always there. Shay sought her advice above that of friends and her parents because she knew that Chloe would never mislead her.

Jill sat up and yawned, her hair a complete mess. She turned suddenly, caught Shay watching her, and said something that Shay couldn't hear.

Shay snatched the plugs from her ears and whispered, "What?"

"I said I'm sorry I woke you."

"You didn't, I was already awake."

Jill grabbed a backpack and started stuffing clothes into it. "I'm going to the campground bathhouse. I need a shower, and I don't want to wake the bears in the back room. Feel free to make coffee or have breakfast."

Jill's bag was packed, and she was out the door before Shay could comment. The mid-April morning was cool, and Jill walked quickly to stave off the chill. She felt a twinge of remorse for not inviting Shay, but it seemed odd to invite someone she barely knew to shower with her, even though they wouldn't be sharing a stall. Guilt turned into aggravation and propelled her faster down the asphalt road.

She felt burdened by Shay, as though it was her job to make sure she had a good time. Jill knew Anne and Ella would do what they always did on trips; they'd socialize with the other campers and soon find a few who would sit around a table and play cards all day. They'd, of course, invite Shay, but Jill knew that her grandmother fully expected her to entertain the woman she'd chosen to invite because she was meddling.

Jill hit the bathhouse door hard, hoping to find it empty since the sun was barely up, but there was humming coming from one of the restroom stalls. She continued on to the shower area, took a spray bottle out of a plastic bag, and liberally sprayed the stall she planned to bathe in with bleach. Then she undressed, slipped her feet into a pair of flip-flops, and dared to step in.

"At least there's good pressure and the water's hot," Jill said lowly as she stepped under the spray and closed her eyes as it enveloped her in warmth. "It is truly sad that the most enjoyable part of this vacation is a shower in a public restroom."

"Pardon?"

Jill's eyes flew open. "I was just talking to myself," she said to the stranger beyond the curtain.

"Good, then you won't mind me chewing myself out for eating an entire pizza last night."

"No, you go right ahead." Jill lathered up her hair with shampoo and rinsed it. She was about to give herself a good scrubbing when she heard a full-blown tirade begin in the next stall.

"I don't know why I do it. I felt full after two slices, but I just kept on eating. I wished Tom would've eaten some of it, then maybe he would've shut the hell up for a few blessed seconds. He went on and on about his boat. It floats, congratulations, now shut your yap. Oh, dear God, I was so close to saying that. And poor Julie, she tried to make him stop flapping his gums because she knew the rest of us were about to kill Tom or ourselves. If I was her, I would've taken him out already, or at least drove off and left him at a rest stop. If Dennis asks them to breakfast this morning, I will divorce him."

Jill scrubbed one arm, unsure if the woman next to her was really talking to herself of if she was expected to respond. "Uh...yeah, no one likes a rattle trap."

"Am I talking too much?"

"No, I meant the guy who wouldn't shut up about his boat," Jill said as she bathed faster.

"I hate camping. When my husband first told me he wanted to buy an RV and tour the country, I thought it was a wonderful idea. Before he retired, I never saw him, but now he's in my face all the time, and I really despise him. I mean I truly hate him. How was I married to him all these years and never noticed that he has a face like an ostrich? Those beady eyes and that bobbing head. His nose looks just like a beak, I swear. And his mother, oh! She calls him every day. The man is sixty-seven, and she still verbally coddles him like a baby. Then she starts in on him about me. I can hear her loud yap clear across the room, which isn't very big because we're in a camper. She..."

The woman went on and didn't notice when Jill switched off the water. Jill dried as fast as she could, but her clothes still clung to her wet skin as she crept out of the stall. Her mouth hung open as the woman continued.

"...I don't know how long I'll go to prison for, but I know serving the sentence will be worth it just to watch that camper burn. Dennis and his mother can live happily ever after, and I'll have my sister send me enough cigarettes so I can barter my way out of being someone's bitch..."

"You sound sleepy, did I wake you up?" Jill asked with concern as she sat beneath a picnic pavilion on her phone, her hair still soaking wet.

Selene's smooth soft voice made Jill long for home. "No, I was just lying on the sofa with a cup of coffee. Sunday morning is my lazy time. How is the happy camper?"

"Campers aren't the joyful lot you think they are. I just chatted with a woman who hates her husband and wants to set their RV on fire."

"It's...not even seven yet. People are awake and pissed off already out there? I think you should rethink this whole vacation thing. You could come stay with me, and I'll keep you very happy."

It was a very enticing offer that warmed Jill from head to toe. "I would love to, but unfortunately, they can't go on without me. Grandma can't see over Sally's steering wheel, and Anne...it's just horrifying to imagine her driving anything."

"What did you do last night?"

"I made fire, we threw meat on it, then we ate it. I drank a few beers and went to bed where I dreamed I was trapped in a store, and I was surrounded by people wanting things I couldn't provide. Care to analyze that?"

Selene laughed. "I think that's self-explanatory. What's on the agenda for today?"

"We're at a campground in north Alabama, and we'll stay here another night unless Grams and Anne decide they want to stay longer. They'll probably make some card-playing buddies and leave me to entertain the friend they've brought along."

"This friend doesn't play cards?" Selene asked.

"She was brought along to keep me company. I found this out yesterday morning when we went to pick up Chloe, and her niece joined us instead."

"So you're babysitting a kid, as well."

Jill pursed her lips as she debated how to answer. She didn't know Selene well enough to ascertain if she was the jealous type, and she didn't want to do or say anything to hamper the good start she felt they had. "Shay is probably around my age. Nevertheless, I still feel like it's a babysitting job."

"Is she a lesbian?"

Jill closed her eyes. "Unfortunately so."

"Ah, so you're being fixed up," Selene said with what Jill felt certain was an edge.

"That's what it would be if I were willing, but I'm not interested in the least."

"You don't have to be defensive."

Jill was sure she didn't sound that way and realized that Selene was testing her. "I only date one woman at a time, and you're the only one I'm interested in seeing."

"I just need to know what I'm up against. Do I need to put on my flannel and boots to hunt you down in the woods?"

Jill laughed. "I could never imagine you wearing that, but if you want to try it on when I get back, I'll be more than happy to watch."

"I actually do have a pair of hiking boots, no flannel, though. I'll model them for you, and you can pick the outfit you want me to wear, or not wear, with them."

"Less is better," Jill agreed with a smile that quickly faded when she spotted Shay jogging by. Shay noticed her, too, and waved. "What're you going to do today?"

"A friend of mine just had a baby, so I'm going to visit her, ooh and ahh over her offspring appropriately, then I plan to spend the rest of the day shopping. That reminds me that my lazy morning is coming to an end. I need to get up and get going. Call me tonight if you have time."

"I will. Enjoy your day."

"You too," Selene said teasingly.

"Mock my pain, go ahead," Jill said with a laugh. "I'll talk to you soon."

Jill blew out a heavy breath when the call ended. She stuffed her phone into her pocket, grabbed her pack, and headed for the campsite with an intense case of homesickness.

Chapter 5

Ella was busy cooking when Jill stepped inside the camper. "Please tell me there's coffee," Jill said as she tossed her pack aside.

"Did you go bathe in one of those germ factories, even though Sally has a perfectly fine shower?" Ella asked with a frown.

"The bathroom with a shower is off your bedroom. I didn't want to wake y'all. Besides, I disinfected the germ den. Where's Anne?"

"She's still sleeping. Shay went out for a jog in case you were wondering."

"I wasn't." Jill poured herself a cup of coffee.

"Don't be mean," Ella said with disapproval in her voice.

"I'm not. I saw her running while I was out. What're we having for breakfast?"

"The rest of us are having a casserole, you're having grits," Ella replied as she peeked into the oven.

"What's with the hostility?"

Ella turned and poked Jill in the chest. "You can be very gracious and polite, but it seems to me that you're going out of your way to be rude to Shay. You hardly spoke to her last night over dinner. This morning, you took off before the sun was barely up."

Jill set her coffee aside. "No one could get a word in edgewise between you and Anne and your rousing conversation about body piercings. I didn't have the nerve to speak up after Anne asked Shay if she'd ever had a nipple ring. I'm sure you

31

missed the fact that I gave Shay the good bed, which is far more comfortable than mine. I also gave her a pair of earplugs so she could block out the symphony of snores coming from your room. Forgive me for not inviting her to take a shower with me. I thought *that* would be rude. And another thing, I would've invited my own friend if I'd known that Chloe wasn't coming with us, but you waited to tell me that at the last minute. Instead, you picked one for me, a stranger that I'm gonna have to get to know whether I like it or not."

Ella jutted her chin. "You're being a shit."

"This little shit berry didn't fall far from the tree," Jill retorted.

"Peter, Paul, and Mary Jenkins, are you two arguing already?" Anne emerged from the bedroom with a string of paper towels woven into a headband and held by bobby pins to keep her hairdo in place.

Ella scowled at Jill. "We're having a spirited discussion."

Anne picked up Jill's coffee cup, took a sip, and sighed happily. "Just like I like it."

"Well, help yourself, I'll just make another," Jill huffed.

Anne took a seat and looked around. "Where's the mute?"

"Anne!" Ella snapped.

"Okay," Anne said, drawing out the word. "But you have to admit, she barely said a word last night even when I tried to draw her into the conversation."

"She's probably jogging back to Baton Rouge." Jill poured herself another cup of coffee. "I know I would if some old woman grilled me about body piercings."

Anne fanned at the air. "Whew, there's a whole lot of bitchiness floating around in here."

"We're on vacation, we're supposed to be having a good time, damn it," Ella ground out, then inhaled deeply. "Let's all just…cool off."

"I am cool," Anne said with a shrug. "So where did you say the mute was again?"

Jill pointed at Anne and smirked at Ella. "Now that's mean."

Shay ran until her legs were rubbery. She looked at her watch and was sad to note that she'd only burned an hour of what was going to be a long day. As she walked and cooled down, she wondered if she rented a car after a few days and went home if anyone would be offended. Anne and Ella looked totally capable of taking care of themselves. The only thing they really needed Jill for was to drive and set up the RV, which looked as though it was on fire as Shay drew closer. She began to run as smoke poured out of one of the windows.

"I told you, Ella, you need to leave more room in your casserole dishes." Anne threw open the door and came face to face with Shay. "Nothing to worry about, hon, except smoke inhalation and smelling like a burned egg for the rest of the day."

Windows started to open all over the camper as Ella and Jill scampered around inside. Shay moved to go in and help, but Anne stopped her. "Trust me, you don't want to go in there. Casserole isn't the only thing burning right now. Jill's ablaze with the red ass."

Shay stared at Anne with her rolled-up paper towels wrapped around her head. "What can I do to help?"

Anne pulled her ringing phone from the pocket of her robe. "You can help me answer this thing. I don't have my glasses on to see the screen."

Shay took the phone. "It's an incoming Facetime call from Dale. Do you want me to accept it?"

"A Face what? Oh, go ahead, he's probably calling me since Ella and Jill aren't answering."

Shay pressed a button, and a man's face filled the screen. He was smiling until he saw Shay. "Oh, hello...isn't this Anne Jacoby's phone?"

"It is, she asked me to answer."

"You must be Chloe's niece. I'm Dale, Ella's son. She isn't answering, so I thought I'd try Anne."

"She's right here." Shay held up the phone for Dale to see Anne.

"Annabelle," he said with a laugh. "Did you just wake up?"

33

Anne squinted at the screen. "Well, I had no idea you could see people when you talk to them. Everyone I've talked to must've been looking at my ear."

"Oh, shit! It's Dad on Facetime," Jill said from inside the camper.

"On what?" Ella asked.

"Why 'oh, shit'? What's 'oh, shit?'" Dale asked. "Jill, where are you?"

Jill came tearing out of the camper and grabbed the phone from Shay. "Hey, Dad. Everything's fine, that was just an excited 'oh, shit.' How're you?"

"I'm good. Your mom just taught me how to use this Face thing. She says you have it on your phone, too, but you didn't answer."

"We were making breakfast." Jill laughed nervously. "I don't even know where my phone is right now."

"Well, let me have a look at Sally."

Anne stuck her face in front of Jill's. "She's on fire right now."

Jill bumped Anne away with her hip and laughed. "You know she's joking."

Dale's face went blank. "Let…let me see her."

"All right, Dad, here's the deal. Grandma baked a casserole, and it leaked over the side of the dish onto the oven burners. That smoked everything up. There's no fire, I repeat no fire." Jill turned the phone away from her face and snarled at Anne. "What is wrong with you?"

"I wanted to see his face when I said that, but I forgot I didn't have my glasses on," Anne said with a shrug.

"Let me see Sally!"

Jill pressed a button on the screen and turned the camera around so Dale could see his precious camper, and she walked inside. Ella was fanning what little smoke was left with a towel. "Your other woman is fine, son," Ella said drolly.

"I'm so glad I got y'all these phones for Christmas. At least now I can see that you're all right," Dale said with a smile.

Ella stuck her face so close to the screen all Dale could see were nostrils. "John Dale Savoy, don't you dare lie to me. We all know what you're really concerned about."

Dale cleared his throat. "Y'all having a good time?"

"Well...we were before the breakfast debacle. Now we're gonna try to eat this casserole." Ella took a good look at the screen. "Son, you need a haircut."

Shay walked into the camper behind Anne and covered her nose because Sally most certainly smelled funky. The next thing she knew, Anne's phone was thrust in her face, and Dale was smiling at her all over again.

"Dale, this is Shay Macaluso, Chloe's niece," Ella said.

Shay smiled and gave a little wave. "Nice to meet you, Dale."

"How do you like my Sally?" Dale asked. "Isn't she a beaut?"

Anne stuck her face in front of the screen again. "She calls it a bus."

When Anne moved away, Dale's face was blank, and Shay began to wave emphatically. "No, I didn't. It's so obviously not a—one of those. I love Sally."

"Dale, honey, we have to go, our breakfast is getting cold." Ella turned the phone toward Jill. "Say goodbye to your father."

Jill waved. "I'm sure I'll see you later on the phone, Dad."

"Wait—"

Jill took the phone from Ella to make doubly sure her father was no longer on the line, then said, "I'm going to choke Mom for teaching him how to use that feature."

Everyone took a shower after breakfast to rid herself of the burned egg smell, including Jill. Anne and Ella did exactly what Jill expected and went to visit their neighbors. Shay sat outside beneath the awning with a book. Jill paced around in the camper annoyed that she didn't feel comfortable pulling out her hammock and stringing it up between two trees, so she could nap half the day away.

Finally, she pushed through the door and gazed at Shay, who was reading. "So you're a nurse."

35

"Yes," Shay replied without looking at her.

"Where do you work?"

Shay closed the book and dropped it on the table. "You sound like you don't believe me."

"I don't know anything about you," Jill said with a shrug. "This is awkward, don't you think?"

"So," Shay said, dragging the word out. "This is your attempt at conversation."

"Yeah," Jill said just as slowly. "I'm not trying to be a dick."

Shay laughed. "Oh, no, you don't have to try at all, it just seems to come so naturally."

"For you, as well." Jill pulled out one of the chairs and sat down as Shay reopened her book. From what she gleaned from the conversation they had the previous night, Shay had been duped into the trip. Jill covered her mouth with her hand to hide her grin as she pondered that Shay thought she was there to be some sort of private nurse to Anne and Ella. Chloe had pulled a big fat fast one, and Jill had always seen her as the sweet and innocent type. No doubt, she'd finally been corrupted by Anne and Ella.

"I'm ready to tell you about Grandma's and Anne's medical conditions," Jill said suddenly.

Shay set her book aside again and gave Jill her full attention.

Jill blew out a breath to keep from laughing. "Anne sometimes has mental lapses and forgets where she's at. She'll wander off if Grandma or I don't corral her. Grandma's memory is all messed up, she tells stories about things that never happened. She has a tendency to fall sometimes. They're just old, that's their problem."

Shay seemed to swallow the lies hook, line, and sinker. "I have to admit, I haven't dealt with real medical issues for a while. I do still remember all my training, so I can help if the need arises."

"What exactly do you do?"

"I'm an RN, but I burned out pretty quick working as a nurse. I discovered laser therapy, and I took some courses. Before I left Utah, I worked with a plastic surgeon as a laser

36

technician. I remove tattoos and unwanted hair, but I also treat scars."

Jill nodded and drummed her fingers on the table. "So if Anne and Grandma get into trouble, you can take the hair out of their butt cracks."

"It amazes me how being a dick comes so easy to you. Unfortunately, there's no laser for that," Shay replied coolly.

Jill laughed. "I was a complete asshole just then, I can't deny it." She cleared her throat. "I apologize. Actually, that sounds like a very interesting line of work."

"What do you do?" Shay asked reluctantly for the sake of conversation.

"I'm a CPA, but I work at the family business, Savoy Steel Works. We manufacture and repair industrial equipment. Basically, I'm a bookkeeper."

"I'm sure being a dick comes in handy when dealing with the IRS."

Jill shook her finger and laughed. "That was a good one. I do appreciate someone who can dish it right back. Do you fish?"

"Yes."

"There's not much to do around here. Do you want to wet a hook?"

"'Fish bite least with wind from the east.' I'm sure you noticed there's a nice easterly breeze blowing through."

"That's a wives' tale. I bet you twenty bucks I'll catch a fish," Jill said cockily. "Within an hour."

"You're on."

"Why does your dad call the camper Sally?" Shay asked as she walked alongside Jill on their way to the lake.

"That's what Dad calls all of his Winnebagos. He's got a naming issue. All of his dogs have a first, middle, and last name. His truck is called Bob, he has a bulldozer named Rex. The computer on his desk is Jezebel because he says it's evil."

Shay nodded. "You have a very interesting family."

"What, yours doesn't have two crazy old women and a man who thinks machinery has a soul?"

"No, we're pretty boring," Shay answered with a smile. "We do have a politician, though. So as far as insanity goes, we may be higher up on the scale. My brother is on the town council where he lives, and he thinks that makes him the right hand of God. My sister believes everything that comes out of his mouth is the gospel. Fortunately, I'm condemned by both of them for being a lesbian."

"What about your parents?"

"I'm the youngest, and they waited until I graduated college to move to Florida. There, they don't have to endure visits from my brother and his incessant preaching. They don't agree with 'the man is the absolute leader of the home' doctrine. They're totally confused by my sexuality, though, and that causes friction. My brother says it's a choice, I know differently. My parents are caught in the middle. They try to be understanding, but invariably, one of them will ask me if I'm gay because I haven't met the right man every time we get together. Chloe is the only truly open mind in my family."

Jill nodded. "Yeah, she and Grandma and Anne like to discuss everything. I had dinner with them one time when they were in the mood to have one of their discussions. I didn't even know what a pansexual was until that night. In two hours' time, they covered health care, baldness in women, traffic congestion, time travel, global warming, and when they got to cunnilingus, I left."

Shay smiled. "Chloe calls their group 'the eternally curious.'"

"She nailed it with that moniker," Jill said with a laugh. "I came out first, then my younger brother, Jude. My parents were accepting, but they didn't want to talk about it too much, but Grams and Anne questioned us like two detectives. They wanted to know about our feelings, the sex, the dynamic of gay and lesbian relationships. Poor Jude nearly had a nervous breakdown."

"The trail to the dock is over there." Shay pointed to a sign when Jill continued in the opposite direction.

"I'm not going to the dock, everyone fishes that spot."

38

Shay's eyes widened when she realized that Jill was headed straight for a thicket. "Should we have brought a machete?"

"Nah," Jill said with a grin. "Just watch your step, there could be snakes."

Shay's stride never slowed, even though Jill fully expected her to turn back. "Snakes always bite the second on the trail," Shay said as she barreled straight into the brush ahead of Jill.

"That's another wives' tale."

"Let's put it to the test." Shay pushed her way through the thicket. "There's some truth in old sayings."

"Yeah, like cats suck out your breath when you're sleeping."

"Most people who have cats know they like to sniff a stinky mouth and sleep near your face. Even though they don't actually suck out your breath, there is reason for that myth. You're second on the trail, so maybe you'll discover why that wives' tale came into existence."

Shay's logic rattled Jill a little, and she started to scan the ground around them intently. She also moved in behind Shay very closely, so a snake would think they were one person. Shay didn't seem intimidated at all; she tromped through the brush without any hesitation until they found the water's edge.

There wasn't much of a bank, but Jill had enough room to stand and cast. She fished her jar of stinky bait out of the tackle box, baited her hook, and set it to go deep. Shay watched with her hands on her hips.

"I'm surprised you even use a float, you strike me as the type of woman who would use the feel method," Shay said.

"I enjoy the thrill of seeing the bobber go under." With a flick of her wrist, Jill sent her line flying and winked. "Besides, you'll be able to watch it, too."

"I am, and it's sideways, which means your bait is lying on the bottom of the lake. You won't even get a nibble like that, not even from a catfish, which is clearly what you're going for."

Jill clamped her lips tightly together as she reeled in her line and sent it flying again. "Do you bait your own hook and take what you catch off the line?"

"Yes, and I clean and cook them, too," Shay said with a cocky smile.

"Do you want to fish? I'll give you my rod after I reel in my catch."

"You can keep your rod to yourself, I don't have a license."

"Neither do I, but I don't think we're gonna be out here long enough for it to matter," Jill said nonchalantly. "I'll have a fish and twenty bucks soon."

Shay tore her gaze from the float and glanced at Jill. "Just so you know, I started the clock on your first cast."

Jill jiggled her rod to make the bait more enticing to any fish that might be passing by it. "What kind of outdoor things do you enjoy?"

"I like to swim, water ski, snowboard in the winter, hiking's okay, but not my favorite. I tried rock climbing, but on my very first outing, someone in our group fell and broke a leg. I didn't see the sense in it after that. What do you like aside from fishing?"

Jill had to think for a moment because that was pretty much all she did on a trip aside from drinking beer and lying in the hammock. "I like motorcycles, dirt bikes mainly. I do have an endorsement on my license, but mostly, I ride off road. There's more mud, and I don't have to worry about some texting jackass plowing over me."

It seemed the catfish were sleeping because time swept by without even a nibble on Jill's line no matter how many times she cast. Shay grew restless and started to explore the bank. Jill watched her as she squatted down and stared at something in the weeds.

"Maybe you should switch to live bait," Shay said as she grabbed at something.

"Did you catch me a frog?" Jill asked with a laugh.

"No, but I think this will be better."

"What the fu—no, Shay!" Jill stumbled backward.

"It's a little water snake, they aren't poisonous. I'll put it on your hook."

"Game over!" Jill practically screamed as she reeled in her line as fast as she could. "Crazy-ass woman digging snakes outta the mud. Put it back—no, throw it way out into the water."

40

Shay waved the snake around as though it was as harmless as a hotdog bun. "I said it isn't poisonous. I wouldn't have picked up a cottonmouth."

"Oh, God…it's wrapped around your wrist." Jill turned away, unable to look at it. "There is something seriously wrong with you!" She went through the brush like a bear on crack, and it took Shay a minute or two to catch up with her.

"Um, I should point out that you lost the bet," Shay said a couple of steps behind Jill.

"You cheated." Jill waved her arm wildly as she marched on. "You don't present someone with a wild animal or reptile when they don't expect it."

"I was offering you bait. Hey, face it, you weren't getting any bites on that smelly stuff you were using. I was helping you."

Jill shook her head. "No, you ran me off the bank on purpose."

"How could I have possibly known that Ms. Super Dyke was afraid of a little ol' water snake?"

Jill whirled around. "Not afraid…sensible."

Shay pursed her lips and gazed into Jill's eyes before saying, "Yeah, that's it."

"You calling me a chicken?"

"If the feathers fit, but we can settle this right now." Shay stuffed her hand into the pocket of her shorts. "I've got the snake in here, he likes the warmth—hey, where're you going?"

"No, I really didn't have a snake in my pocket," Shay said with a grin as she and Ella made lunch.

"Oh, I wish I'd been there to see her face. Anne is going to die laughing when she's finished being fleeced by the card shark in the next camper. To be fair, Jill isn't afraid of much, but she does not like snakes. That probably comes from being chased around the yard with one by her older brothers when they were little. Will and Seth were always tormenting her." Ella waved a finger. "I told Dale and Viv having all those children so close together would be a handful, but they just kept making them

41

every two years. What did I know? I only ever gave birth to one."

"Where is Anne, by the way?" Shay asked with concern.

"I just said she's next door, why are you looking at me like that?"

Shay set the lettuce that she'd been washing aside and dried her hands, wondering if Ella had forgotten about Anne's periods of confusion. "I should go over there. She could get confused and go to the wrong campsite or wander off."

"Hold on a minute. What're you talking about?"

"Jill told me that Anne has mental lapses and sometimes forgets where she is. We're in unfamiliar surroundings, and I'm afraid that Anne might get lost."

Ella stared at her a moment, then snorted. "Sugar, she may have the mouth of a sailor and the tact of a hooker, but there is one thing Anne Jacoby is not, and that's senile. You've been played. What did she tell you about me?"

"That you have memory loss, and the stories you tell aren't real."

Ella put a hand to her chest and gazed out the window at Jill, who was sleeping in her hammock with a cowboy hat covering her face. "That little liar. I'm gonna go out there right now and spray her down with the hose."

Shay inhaled sharply. "No, don't. This kind of retaliation deserves some serious thought and planning."

"I want in."

Shay nodded. "I'll let you know when I come up with something." She resumed washing the lettuce. "Does Anne have kids?"

"No, she really wanted them, though. Chester was sterile, and it was heartbreaking for both of them. She considers Dale her son, too, and my grandchildren and great-grandchildren are hers, as well. She's been at my side for the birth of every single one of them. That's saying something, you know? Friends like that…well, they're family, plain and simple."

"When Chloe first told me about y'all, I thought you were really sisters because that's how she refers to you."

"She is my sister. That woman and I have been through good times and plenty of bad. She's my rock. She lost Ches two years before John died. John loved her too, so much. He gave Anne time to grieve, then sat her down at the kitchen table and told her that he wanted her to move in with us. John had a caretaker's personality, he always made sure those around him had whatever they needed." Ella folded her arms and stared out the window. "I think he knew he was right behind Ches and wanted to make sure that Anne and I were set and happy. Jill is a lot like her grandfather, except she's a devious little liar."

They watched as Anne came walking around the neighboring camper and crept over to where Jill was sleeping. Very carefully, she lifted the hat, and before Jill could fully awaken, she planted a big kiss right on her mouth. Jill flailed and hollered as Anne scampered away laughing hysterically.

Chapter 6

Jill had to silently, begrudgingly admit that watching the square dancers was kind of entertaining. They looked like they ranged in age from their thirties to possibly seventy. They twirled, stomped, yelled, and do-si-doed. Every third song, they invited someone in the audience to dance with them. The dancers looked like they were having fun, but Jill had to wonder what kind of person suddenly decided one day, "Hey, I wanna join a square dancing group." Was there a call for it in the paper? Were there websites, or was it a thing passed down from one generation to the next? She'd seen ads for belly dancing classes to lose weight, but she'd never seen one that said "swing your partner round and round if you want to lose those pounds."

Anne bumped Jill and said, "Are you drunk?"

"No, I only had one beer with dinner, why?"

"Because you're staring into space with your head cocked to the side, and you look like you're about to drool," Anne said with a grin. "Quit sitting there like a knot on a log and clap your hands, you might have some fun."

"Yeah, clapping always perks me up." Jill looked down at Shay, who was seated on the other side of Ella, and laughed. Shay was clapping along to the music because she had to. Every time she stopped, Ella would grab her hands and start smashing them together.

When the music ended, the spokesman for the group walked down into the audience, which only consisted of a dozen people. "Who wants to cut a rug with us?" he asked with a heavy country accent as he gazed at the crowd.

To Jill's utter horror, Anne started waving her arms and yelled, "Come get these young'uns sitting with us, they're full of energy." Jill looked at Shay, who had flushed deep red and was about to crawl out of her chair. Jill didn't have that many shy bones, but the two she did have began to rattle, and she knew how mortified Shay must've felt. So before the polyester cowboy could get to them, Jill jumped up and sacrificed herself. She raced over to him and told a lie on Shay's behalf.

"My friend has a bad knee, so you're just stuck with me."

"Bullshit, I'm ready to shake a leg," Anne said behind her.

They were led to the stage with a round of applause. Underneath hot lights that made Jill immediately sweat, the spokesman conducted an interview. "What's your name, and where're you from, sugar?" he asked and stuck the microphone in Jill's face.

"Umm...Jill...from Baton Rouge," she said, and her voice echoed beneath the pavilion.

Anne didn't wait to be asked and grabbed the mic out of the cowboy's hand. "I'm Anne, and I'm from Baton Rouge. How y'all doin'?" That elicited another round of applause, and Anne didn't return the microphone when the cowboy reached for it. "I've never square danced before, but I have juked and jived to some big band music. Some of you look old enough to remember Harry Potter."

There was no applause, but Jill could hear a few crickets chirp and some confused mumbles as she covered her face with her hands.

"Glenn Miller, Anne, dear God," Ella cried.

"That's right," Anne said. "I don't know why I get those boys confused. Maybe it's because their names rhyme."

Jill leaned in close to Anne and whispered, "They do not rhyme, what's wrong with you?"

The spokesman managed to get the microphone back from Anne and said, "Ladies, you just follow our lead, and we're gonna show you a good time."

Everyone took his or her place, and Jill realized that her partner was a six-foot cowboy with shoulders almost as wide. The music started, and he dragged her around like a ragdoll. At times, she felt her feet leave the floor. The dance only lasted a couple of minutes, but to Jill, it felt like an hour in a chiropractor's office. Anne was hooting and hollering, and when the music stopped, she didn't. She shuffled off the low stage swinging her arm around like she had a lasso in it, while Jill was forced to take a bow.

"Thank you," Shay said later as they walked back to their campsite.

Jill purposely walked slow, giving Anne and Ella a wide lead. The pair was arm in arm and stopped every so often to cut a jig. The urge to choke Anne was still too powerful, and Jill needed some space.

"I could tell by the way you looked that you were ready to bolt." Jill stuffed her hands into her pockets.

"No, my legs wouldn't move, but I was ready to puke. I once failed a history class in high school because the teacher required us to stand up and read our reports." Shay shook her head. "I couldn't do it. I'd get light-headed at just the thought. Public speaking or being on some sort of display is a phobia of mine that I wish I had the strength to change."

"I wish I had one artistic bone in my body. I'd love to be able to sing, play an instrument, or paint." Jill sighed. "My talent is in numbers. I always had math honors in school, and that branded me an egghead. I had a huge crush on this girl who could sing in high school, and I was never really sure if I was drawn to her or her voice. My eyes would tear during her performances because it was just so beautiful. I wanted that ability, to be able to open my mouth and make people swoon."

"Have you ever tried to sing?" Shay asked.

"Oh, yeah, and I even talked my mom into letting me have voice lessons. The music teacher gave them after school. I went to one session, and I'll never forget the look on her face when I began to squawk. She very kindly explained to me that everyone had talents, and I needed to continue to search for mine."

Shay laughed. "You hit a high note today when I showed you that snake."

"Has anyone ever explained to you that those things aren't meant to be picked up? It pisses them off."

"I have a lot of experience. My parents owned a plant nursery when I was growing up. Dad taught me, my brother, and sister how to identify poisonous snakes, and it was our job to relocate the nonpoisonous kind when they found their way into the customer areas."

"My dad just made me wash his truck." Jill watched as Anne mimicked a square dancing move. "Harry Potter does not rhyme with Glenn Miller. She's just nuts."

"Yeah, she is," Shay said with a smile. "But she makes me laugh."

"They make each other laugh, look at them." Jill smiled as Anne took Ella by the hand, and they started doing the twist, or some variation thereof.

"They're full of vitality, that's for sure."

"They are full of something, yes," Jill said with a laugh.

Shay glanced at her. "They absolutely adore you."

"I know, and the love is very much mutual. They've always been my go-to girls. I can tell them anything, and I trust their advice because they know me better than anyone. My only complaint is that they meddle in my love life. They've tried to fix me up before, and it was a disaster. They also have to meet any woman I date, and God help her if they don't approve."

"What happens if they don't like her?" Shay asked.

"They're aloof, dismissive, and sometimes downright rude. Anne asked a woman I was seeing how much she paid for her cleavage. I was so mad I couldn't speak for almost five minutes, and I haven't brought anyone else to meet them lately. The only one they ever really liked was Jeri, and she was my first serious girlfriend. We met in college and were together for eleven years."

"That's a long time."

"We had a good run," Jill said with a sigh. "We were both nineteen when we met, and I fell completely head over heels. Jeri was so driven, she grew up dirt poor, and she was determined to make something of herself. She pushed me, too. I graduated with an accounting degree, but she insisted that I

47

become a CPA, and I did, even though I didn't want it. My future was basically carved in stone, which was the family business. Jeri's goals were clear-cut. She wanted to be a dermatologist, and she wanted her own clinic in New Mexico, of all places, and that's exactly where she is now."

"You didn't want to go with her?"

"By the time she finished school, I had realized that I did enjoy working with my family. Dad relied on me, and we were making things happen. The business was doing better than it ever had before, and I took some credit for that. Dad and I had financial strategies that we were working out, and I didn't want to pack up and leave when Jeri found the position in New Mexico. Incidentally, that's why she wanted me to go for the CPA, so I would have better opportunities when she was ready to make her move. She'd planned our whole future, and I felt manipulated, even though I was fully aware of what she was doing. Anyway, we tried the long-distance thing for a while before we both accepted that it was over."

Shay wrapped her arms around herself. "Do you have regrets?"

"Yes and no." Jill unzipped her hoodie, took it off, and draped it over Shay's shoulders. "I've just resigned myself to accepting that's how things were supposed to work out. She wouldn't have been happy here, and I wouldn't have been happy there. Some fairytales don't last forever. I think you should tell me your story now."

Shay pulled the hoodie from her shoulders when they arrived at the camper and handed it to Jill. "Thanks for this, but I'm kind of tired."

Jill nodded. "You go on then. I have a call to make. Good night."

"Night, Jill."

Shay watched Jill disappear into the darkness, then went inside. The door to the bedroom Ella and Anne shared was closed and afforded her a bit of privacy. As Shay readied for bed, she contemplated the fact that there was no story to tell Jill. Behind her was a long string of failed relationships, and she couldn't say she truly mourned the loss of any of them. She

48

wholeheartedly agreed with Jill about fairytales and their short life.

"I square danced tonight."

"Oh," Selene said with a laugh, "and you admitted it. What other exciting things have you done?"

Jill snorted with laughter. "That was the highlight. I'm dying out here."

"Poor baby. What're you going to follow the dancing up with—quilting?"

Jill whimpered. "Maybe."

"A week is plenty of time in the woods. Hold out until then, and just tell them you've had enough. You're the one behind the wheel, you have the control."

"If this was anyone else besides my grandmother and Anne, I would consider doing that. I can't disappoint them."

All merriment had faded from Selene's tone when she said, "Surely, they realize you're a grown woman who has a life of her own."

"They do, but this extended road trip is probably gonna be their last. I want them to be able to do what they want to do, and sadly, tonight, it was square dancing."

"Did you dance with Shay?" Selene asked lightly.

"No, that's not her kind of party," Jill said and suppressed a yawn.

"How do you wash your clothes?"

"Sally has a small washer and dryer."

"Sally?" Selene said. "Who is that?"

"The Winnebago we're traveling in. Long story, but my dad likes to name inanimate objects."

"Ah, that makes perfect sense. The copier at our office is named Hateful Bitch. What else did you do today?"

"I napped and did a little fishing."

"I'm jealous of the napping."

"You don't enjoy fishing?" Jill asked with a smile.

"Not even a little bit. My dad took me once, but I refused to touch the bait, and I got mad when I sat there longer than a

49

minute and nothing happened. It's very boring. I prefer indoor activities, and I'd like to enjoy them with you."

Selene's comment made a direct hit, and Jill felt her body respond. "I'll come see you as soon as I get back into town."

"Do you...share a bed with Shay? I don't like competition, especially when I haven't had a chance to make a play."

"There's no one else on the field, just you and me," Jill said with a smile.

"You scored a point with that response. I have to go to bed now because I have to get up early in the morning. I will be thinking of you, though."

"I'll be doing the same."

"I doubt you will with a camper full of people," Selene said seductively. "Good night, Jill."

Jill caught the innuendo after the call ended and groaned. She walked slowly back to the campsite in a lust-filled daze. When she returned to the camper, what awaited her inside tore her from her haze.

"I need to go, Ches is waiting on me," Anne said as she paced back and forth.

Ella looked mortified as Shay tried to reason with Anne. "You're right where you need to be. Look, here's Jill, we're camping together, remember?"

Anne stared at Jill as though she were a stranger. "I don't know who that is."

"What's going on?" Jill asked with concern.

"We'd gone to bed, and all of the sudden, Anne said she saw Ches walk out of the room. She doesn't know where she is."

Ella's acting was superb, but Anne was going for the Oscar. She stared at the refrigerator and said, "Ches, honey, are you hungry? I'll make you something. What do you want?"

"Anne," Shay said in a soothing tone. "Why don't you sit down and Ella will make Ches something to eat?"

Anne sank down on Jill's bed looking dazed and confused. "I didn't go grocery shopping, and he loves capers on his salad. I should run and get some."

"No, we have capers. I'll get them," Ella said and pretended to dig around in one of the cabinets.

50

"What's going on with her?" Jill asked.

"I called an ambulance, they'll be here soon," Shay whispered. "Until the paramedics arrive, we need to keep her very calm. Talk to her, be comforting, and try to help her understand where she is."

"Hey," Jill said nervously with a smile. "You sure cut a rug tonight at the square dancing...thing. Did you have fun?"

Anne stared at Shay with a blank expression. "Who the hell are you?"

"I'm Jill, your adopted granddaughter. You taught me how to tie my shoes. You used to read to me. Granted, they were trashy romance novels, and you put fairytale characters in place of the ones in the books. For a long time, I pictured Dopey with heaving bosoms."

Anne shook her head slowly. "You're the neighbor's kid that stole all the plums off my tree."

Jill stood abruptly. "Okay, this is horse shit. Y'all are screwing with me because I made up a bunch of crap and told it to Shay."

"Go outside and wait for the ambulance," Ella snapped. "Go!"

Jill looked truly stunned. For a moment, she waited for one of them to crack, but they held to their parts in the mock drama. "Anne, you know me," she said with desperation.

"That's right, I do," Anne said dreamily. "You're a lying little shit, haha."

Jill's shoulders sagged. "Oh, you are all assholes," she breathed out.

"Just be thankful I wasn't able to find another snake. It would've been in your bed along with Anne's fart," Shay said with a grin and gave Jill a little shove. "Gotcha."

51

Chapter 7

Jill awoke just as Shay walked out the door the next morning. She sat up and peered through the blinds as Shay stretched her legs. Shay was dressed in a pair of yoga pants and a sweatshirt, and Jill did have to mentally concede that Shay had a rather nice backside.

"Why don't you run with her?"

"Why are you up so early?" Jill turned from the window and regarded Ella. "Wait, I'm not speaking to you."

"You deserved what you got, and it could've been worse. Anne wanted to pour ketchup all over herself and claim she was attacked by a bear." Ella threw up her hands. "Why would you lie to Shay like that?"

"Oh, you've got your nerve," Jill said with a derisive laugh. "I was just messing with her, and after she tried to follow Anne around, I was gonna tell her the truth. But what you and Chloe did makes my little prank pale in comparison. She thinks she's here as your personal nurse. I'm surprised you and Anne aren't limping around and acting feeble."

"I didn't tell her anything of the sort, nor did I imply it," Ella said firmly. "I don't know what Chloe said to get her to come with us. I assumed that Shay wanted to take this trip."

"Uh-huh, your eyes get puffy when you lie a lot."

"There's something in the air here that's irritating my sinuses, that's why I'm ready to move on." Ella grabbed the coffeepot and filled it with water. "What time do you think you'll have Sally set for the road?"

Jill glanced at her watch. "We'll be rolling out of here before noon, unless you feel the need to leave sooner."

"No, that's perfect. Anne and I took your computer to bed with us last night, and we think we'd like to avoid the more touristy places like Lookout Mountain and Ruby Falls."

"But I thought those were exactly the places you wanted to go," Jill said, taken aback.

"We can always go to those places on the way home. We'll put it to a vote, but we'd like you and Shay to see what we've found first."

Jill threw up a hand and let it drop onto the bed. "We don't have to vote. Now that you've rearranged everything, I don't really care where we go."

"Shay has a say-so, too, so we'll present the idea to her when she gets back. Blueberry pancakes sound good to you?"

A smile spread across Jill's face. "Absolutely."

"Good, get dressed and go down to the camp store. They had some pretty berries on a display next to the checkout counter yesterday. Take the scooter, it'll be quicker."

Jill grunted. "Beware the grandmother offering treats. There's always a catch."

"Jill doesn't need my help. Ella and Anne have as much energy as I do." Shay walked along the road with her phone pressed to her ear. "I think that old skin is a disguise for two very healthy teenagers. I'm thinking about renting a car and driving home. Do you think they'll be seriously offended?"

"Aren't you having a good time?" Chloe asked with desperation on the fringes of her tone.

"Honestly, this isn't the right time for me to take a vacation. I need to—"

"It's the perfect time. You're unemployed, and when you get a new job, it's going to be a while before you can take any appreciable time off," Chloe argued.

Shay stopped walking. "I need you to be totally honest with me. Is my staying with you becoming a pain in the ass?"

"Oh, Shay, of course not. You've only been here a month, and your company has been extremely welcome and enjoyable.

You think I tricked you into going away because you were getting on my nerves, don't you?"

"You know, when you live alone for a while, you get set in your ways, and—"

"Oh, no! Nothing like that. Honey, you could live with me from here on out if you wanted to. I love having you here. I wanted you to get to know Jill. She's a nice single woman, and you're single now, and—"

"Wait, are you trying to hook me up with her?" Shay squeaked. "Is that really why you convinced me to go?"

"Well, it's a lot of things. You were stressed before you told Chris the relationship was over, then there was that terrible fight, and you had to leave before you'd planned. You were frazzled when you got here, you've seemed depressed, you had all those problems with the state and your license," Chloe said rapid-fire, sounding more nervous by the second. "You needed a vacation, time to get yourself back together, and Ella felt that you and Jill would really enjoy each other's company."

Shay rubbed her forehead with the back of her hand and began walking again. "Ella is going to be sorely disappointed. I'm not the least bit interested in Jill, and she seems annoyed that I'm here. Does she know y'all are trying to hook us up?"

"Okay, there's not a y'all. Ella was the one that wanted you two to meet. I'm the one that wanted you to have a nice vacation. I'm one hundred percent certain that she did not tell Jill her intentions because Jill would've outright refused to go on the trip. She doesn't like to be fixed up."

"Well, that cinches it. I'll make arrangements to pick up a rental car today."

"Whatever you think is best, honey," Chloe said in her most placating tone.

"I have to go now. There's some idiot coming right at me on a scooter. Love you, bye."

"Need a ride?" Jill asked as she stopped alongside Shay.

"No, I'm fine, thanks," Shay said and stuffed her phone into her pocket.

"Did I interrupt your call?"

"No, I was just checking on Chloe. Where are you going?"

54

"To the camp store. Grandma saw blueberries there, and she wants some for the pancakes. Hey, look, we're gonna be moving out this morning, so if you want to eat and shower, you may want to get a move on. Sure you won't change your mind about the ride? By the time you jog all the way to the camping spurs, I will have already been to the store and back."

Shay blew out a breath. "All right."

Jill scooted up farther on the seat. "You're gonna want to hold on to my waist. There's nothing behind you to hang on to."

"I'll be fine," Shay said as she climbed on and clamped her hands on either side of the seat.

"If you lose your balance, you could make us both fall."

"I do not want to hold you," Shay snapped.

Jill slowly turned and looked over her shoulder. "Do I smell bad or something?"

"I'm the one that stinks. I'm a sweaty nasty mess. You really don't want me that close to you right now. Take my word for it."

"Just hold on to my waist, you don't have to hug me," Jill said as she took off slowly.

Shay gritted her teeth as Jill puttered along at a snail's pace. She was livid with Chloe and the fact that she was in Alabama preparing to go farther north when she really needed to be home and getting her life in order. "Does this thing go any faster?"

"Oh, yeah, it'll fly, I just don't want to fling you off the back. It would be ironic that the one of us who knows first aid would be lying in a puddle on the road."

Shay stared at the back of Jill's head and mentally went off on her. You are a cocky shit...dick. I can't believe Chloe would think I could ever be interested in someone like you. You may be good-looking, but you've got all the charm of a porcupine.

Jill glanced over her shoulder. "You okay back there?"

"Fine."

Another thought struck Shay hard and incensed her even more. Maybe Jill did know that Ella was trying to fix them up, and she'd purposely chosen to be an asshole. That was rejection with an added insult.

"You wanna stop digging your fingers into my hips? It feels like you're trying to squeeze my bones out."

55

"I'm just holding on tight like you told me to," Shay said with a sardonic smile.

Jill parked in front of the store and waited for Shay to get off the scooter before she did. Silently, they walked inside, and Jill noticed the berries that Ella had mentioned. Shay went the opposite direction and wandered the aisles.

"Those are greenhouse berries," the woman behind the counter said when Jill picked up a carton. "They come from a local farm up the road. They're organic, but they're a little bitter for my tastes. They'll be fine in muffins, though."

"And pancakes?" Jill asked as she sniffed at them.

"Oh, definitely. I think it's fair to warn folks what they're getting. We have wonderful blueberries here, but they're not ripe yet. My husband has a little farm, too, but he doesn't grow them year-round in a greenhouse like these people do. Personally, I think the ones grown outside are much better, so don't judge us by these berries."

"Well, they're going straight into pancake batter," Jill said distractedly as she looked around for Shay, then she heard a groan. "I'll be right back."

She found Shay in the candy aisle clutching several bags of licorice. "Look at this," Shay said. "They have grape and green apple. You don't find this everywhere."

"Well, grab a bunch and let's go."

Shay took two steps and froze. "I don't have my wallet."

"So," Jill said with a shrug. "Chloe gave Ella your grocery money."

"What?" Shay exclaimed and tossed the candy back onto the rack. "I may not have a job right now, but I'm not destitute. I can pay my own way."

"Ms. Unemployed and Proud, grab the licorice and let's go."

"No." Shay moved past her and walked out of the store.

"And you're hard-headed," Jill said as she grabbed several bags of each flavor and took them to the register.

When she walked out, Shay was seated on the scooter, arms folded with her head lolled back. "You want to drive?" Jill asked. "It's easy, the transmission is automatic."

56

"Sure. Whatever, let's go." Shay turned the key and took off before Jill was situated.

"Hang on a minute, are you trying to kill me?" Jill hollered.

"That is on my list of things to do," Shay said as she stopped.

Jill hit her in the chest with the bag. "Hold this while I get both ass cheeks on this seat. I was being nice by letting you drive, and I don't normally do that. This scooter is like a tricycle, any idiot can handle it, but I guess I was wrong about that!"

Shay looked into the bag and yelled, "There's licorice in here! I told you I didn't want it!"

Jill climbed right back off the scooter and faced Shay. "What is your problem?"

"You!" Shay twirled a finger. "And all of this. The state *misplaced* my RN license files, and I should be in Baton Rouge hounding them to find them, so I can go back to work, so I can get a place of my own, so I can begin my life again. Instead, I'm out traipsing around in the woods all because Chloe and your grandmother wanted to play matchmaker. They could've introduced us at home, and I could've turned my nose up at your narcissistic ass then," Shay practically screamed and shook the bag in her hand. "But no, I'm stuck out here with you and licorice I specifically said I did not want!"

Jill slowly raised a finger and spoke calmly. "I am not a narcissist. Hear me when I say that I don't want to be out here any more than you do. I'm just as pissed at the crappy Cupids as you are. I'm actually seeing someone, and I could be home with something far more exciting than a scooter between my legs right now. I won't deny that I was…kind of a dick to you at first because I thought you were in on the whole matchmaking scheme. Now that I know differently, I'm trying to be nice."

"My head feels like it's gonna explode." Shay squinted and pinched the bridge of her nose. "My life is so out of my control right now, I do not need this added stress."

"You have another headache?"

Shay nodded and closed her eyes.

57

"You want me to go back into the store and get you something for it?"

"No, it'll subside when I calm down, but thanks." Shay took a few calming breaths. "I need to ask you a favor."

"Well, like I said, I'm being nice now." Jill set her hands on her hips. "What do you need?"

"When we leave here, would you take me to the closest airport, so I can rent a car and go home?"

"Hell no," Jill said with a laugh. "If I'm stuck on this trip, you are too."

Shay opened one eye and glared at her.

"That was a joke. Yeah, I'll take you, but let's get one thing clear. I'm not a narcissist."

Anne's head was pressed to Ella's as they listened to Chloe recount the conversation she'd had with Shay. "So she's planning to come home," Chloe said with resignation. "Over the past year when we've talked, her voice has grown steadily dull. She doesn't have any more spark, she's not the exuberant woman I've always known. I've tried talking to her about it, but there's always an excuse. 'I'll be better when I straighten out things with Chris. I'll be fine when work slows down. I'll be okay once this mess with my license is worked out.' She's just not managing stress like she used to. I think she's simply worn down and won't admit it. That's why I wanted her to take the trip before she found another job."

"Okay, don't worry," Ella soothed. "I'll stab Anne in the hand or do something that will require Shay's attention."

"Or you could just reason with the woman," Anne said and folded her hands behind her back. "Chloe, Ella can do that, you know she's good at it."

"I hope y'all will talk her out of coming back. She needs the rest."

"Leave it to us," Ella reassured. "I hear them outside, we'll talk to you soon." She ended the call and stared at the screen. "Look at that, there's a speaker button—oh, now it's gone. I don't understand this phone at all."

"We're back," Jill announced as she opened the door. "And it's time for a meeting, but first, I need to talk to you alone," she said to Ella.

Anne gazed up at the ceiling. "Someone's in trouble."

Chapter 8

"Pour some of the berries into the batter and stir gently," Anne said as she fried bacon.

The noise of the food cooking made it even more difficult to try to decipher what was being said behind the closed door of the bedroom. Ella's and Jill's voices were raised for a moment, and Shay was attempting to eavesdrop unsuccessfully. Anne switched on a fan and opened a window, which pretty much squashed Shay's chances of hearing anything else.

"Have you ever watched any of those old war movies?" Anne asked out of the blue.

"One or two," Shay said as she stirred the batter.

"Then you know they have the fighting men up front in the heat of the battle. Somewhere behind them is some general looking at the big picture. He's not being pummeled or shot at, his head is cool, and he's making all the decisions, or at least that's how I think it goes. The men on the front line can't think about anything else but fighting and surviving, so they can't see what needs to be done. Are you following me?"

Shay blinked a few times as she stirred the berries into the batter. "I think so."

"We talked to Chloe. She told us you want to go home. She also told us that you've been on the front lines for a while, and you need time to think. So give it a few more days. You'll make Chloe happy, you'll be more rested and clear-headed, and we'll use Jill's computer to find a cheap flight. You'll be home in a few hours, and the next day, you can hit the bricks running."

"Anne, I—"

"Look, Ella's bright idea to keep you with us is stabbing me in the hand. I'm ninety-nine percent certain that she wasn't serious, but there's that one percent that has me nervous." Anne chuckled. "Help an old woman out."

Shay had cooled down some, but she was still resolved to going home. "I've basically taken a month off to get my crap together because I didn't intend to leave Utah as quickly as I did. I need structure, a job, a schedule to feel normal again. Being on vacation right now is actually adding to my stress."

"I can understand that," Anne said with a nod. "How about we make a deal? Stay three more days, then go home. I admire your fighting spirit, and I'd like to get to know you better."

"Anne—"

"It's only a week."

"You said three days."

Anne shrugged. "I'm old, I get confused."

Shay chewed her bottom lip as she mulled the request. Her hopes of continuing her work in laser therapy were dimming. People could attend a few courses and be certified as a laser tech, and prospective employers were less interested in paying the salary of an RN when they could get someone else at a much cheaper rate, regardless of experience. Shay had pretty much resigned herself to having to go back into typical nursing, and she wasn't looking forward to it.

"I'll give you three or four days and see how I feel," she said with a sigh.

The bedroom door opened just as Shay was beginning to pour the pancake batter on the griddle. Ella approached her looking contrite and said, "Hon, I owe you an apology. I—"

"Zip it, she's staying," Anne said. "Just say you're sorry."

"I call this meeting to order," Ella announced as they ate breakfast. "Anne and I talked last night, and we thought it might be interesting if we did some nontypical things on this trip, so we came up with some ideas. We'll put it to a vote, but we'd like to go to Paul's Bigfoot Safari. They have their own campground. What do y'all say?"

61

Jill grimaced and scratched the back of her neck as she glanced at Shay. "Doesn't Bigfoot live in Oregon?"

"The Foot is everywhere," Anne said. "They even spotted him at Honey Island Swamp, and that's not far from us." She raised her hand. "I vote yes."

All eyes settled on Shay then. "I'm…uh…okay with that."

Jill shrugged. "Let's go see Bigfoot then."

"Oh, I knew you two would be onboard, that's why we made the reservations last night," Ella said excitedly. "It's gonna be so much fun. They take you out into the woods on a mule, but it's not an animal, it's a camouflaged golf cart, and you get to wear night-vision goggles."

Jill's head lolled back. "And yet we went through the pretense of a meeting."

Anne gave her a playful nudge. "It's good to let the monkey think it has some control every now and then."

Jill had no idea that green apple licorice could be so delicious. She held out her hand palm up and said, "Green me." Shay slapped a braided piece into it, and Jill stuck it into her mouth.

All the secrets and lies were out of the box, and Jill was more relaxed. Shay wasn't interested in her, either, and she felt free to get to know Shay on her own terms. What little she knew, she liked thus far. Shay had a quick wit and a "don't screw with me" attitude, and she was shaping up to be a decent co-pilot. She kept Jill supplied with treats and assisted in berating other drivers.

Anne and Ella were seated in the back with Jill's laptop, combing the net for roadside oddities when Ella said suddenly, "I've accidentally hit one of your little picture things on the top of the screen, and it opened a new page. I just can't see you in a red patent leather strap-on harness. Do they have other colors?"

"Grams! Close that! Close it!" Jill sputtered. "Respect my privacy."

Ella completely ignored her and stared at the screen. "Would you look at that, Anne, this dildo says it warms and vibrates."

Anne cocked her head. "Jill, do you ever worry that it'll malfunction and blow up your vagina or the one you're using it on?"

Jill released a guttural growl and gripped the steering wheel tighter. Shay sank low in her seat, covered her face with her hands, and laughed hysterically.

"We want to know about this, Jillian. I've never seen anything like it in my life," Ella said excitedly.

"Yes, you have," Anne said with a snort. "It just wasn't purple swirl or rubber. Frankly, I would've gone with the blue, that's my favorite color."

"What does a bullet do?" Ella asked. "I assume they're not talking about the kind you shoot. Oh, wait, it's a vibrator, a little vibrator, and you put it in this pocket on the harness. How ingenious."

Anne and Ella cocked their heads and stared at something on the screen. Anne looked disappointed when she said, "I don't think I have one of those. Monkey, where is the G-spot, and what do you do with it?"

Shay looked like she was having convulsions in the passenger's seat as she laughed.

"Stop acting so naïve," Jill said. "I've seen the books y'all read."

"They don't come with pictures, though," Anne said with her eyes glued to the screen, and Ella was steadily pressing keys.

Anne tapped the screen. "That goes in the butt."

"How do you know that?" Ella asked.

"Because it says it goes in the butt. Jill, have you ever tried that?"

Jill slapped the steering wheel with a scowl and glanced at Shay. "There's nothing sacred with them."

"Women are so much more in tune with their bodies nowadays," Ella said casually. "They're not afraid to explore sexually pleasurable things. I wish we would've been born in this age. I didn't even know we were supposed to have orgasms. That was something my mother never discussed with me."

Anne shook her head. "No, in our day, sex wasn't about our enjoyment, it was just a duty. Jill—"

63

"No! No more questions. If you want to learn something, read. That's what y'all used to tell me."

"You were no help at all, Shay," Jill said as they sat in the camper while Ella and Anne checked them into the Bigfoot camp.

"I really couldn't breathe. I swallowed a whole braid of licorice." Shay scrubbed at her eyes. "You may want to clear the history on your browser because they were on a BDSM site just before we got here."

Jill watched as Shay pulled another piece of licorice from the pack and held out her hand. "What made you change your mind about leaving?"

"I didn't." Shay set a piece of candy in Jill's palm. "I told Anne I'd give it a few days while I thought about it." Shay chomped on the licorice and looked out the window. "I hope this place doesn't make me regret that."

Jill looked at all the netting and camouflage tarps strung up in the trees. "What the hell have we let them get us into?"

"These people are serious," Shay said as she looked at a sign bearing the camp rules.

No loud music at any time.

Food must be stored and sealed at all times.

No weapons of any kind allowed.

No laser lights, Q beams, ever.

All expeditions are escorted by Paul's employees. Hunting on your own will result in immediate expulsion from the compound.

If you encounter Bigfoot, for your own protection, lie on the ground face down and remain still.

Tips and cameras are welcome.

Anne and Ella bounded out of the command center. Ella had papers in her hand, and Anne was wearing a chain around her neck with a plastic foot dangling from it. She held it up along with a small bag as she climbed into the camper. "They give these to all the hunters. Y'all wanna wear yours now?"

Shay chewed her bottom lip for a second before saying, "I'm afraid I might break it. I'll put mine somewhere safe."

Jill was less reserved. "I'm not wearing a Bigfoot foot around my neck."

"You're a party pooper just like your grandmother," Anne said with a scowl.

Ella started handing Jill pieces of paper. "This is the map to our site. This is an expanded copy of the rules. This is the card that goes on Sally's windshield. This is our reservation for the hunt tonight at ten."

"Are you serious?" Jill asked. "Y'all are gonna stay up late to hunt an imaginary creature."

"You better watch your tone," Anne warned. "You don't want to piss off people dressed in black with guns strapped to their hips."

"Are you kidding me?" Jill asked aghast. "They're armed?"

Ella nodded. "Even the woman that checked us in. She said it was just one of those stunner things, and it was for our protection."

Shay rolled her eyes. "I feel so much safer."

"Let's get to our site," Anne said. "I'm gonna need a nap before the hunt...and lunch."

"Do you wish you would've gotten that rental car this morning?" Jill whispered as Anne and Ella settled into their seats.

Shay nodded. "Uh-huh."

Jill had seen many campgrounds, but her jaw sagged, and her foot slipped off the gas pedal twice. Sally rolled on slowly as she stared at the cadre of camouflaged vehicles and tents. One man sat atop his RV in a lawn chair, his binoculars trained on the woods beyond.

"They really do take this seriously," Shay whispered in awe. "This is like a militaristic zone."

Jill backed into a slip covered with a quilt of netting and camouflage tarps strung from the trees high overhead. "What is the reason for all of this?" she asked.

"The campground is designed to blend in with nature to be more welcoming to the Bigfoot," Anne explained. "That's what they told us when we checked in."

"Oh, is that it? Well, let me just craft a banner that says, 'We come in peace or bite-sized pieces,'" Jill said with a sardonic laugh.

"Look at it this way, the covering does provide shade," Ella added happily. "There's always a positive."

"I've seen some gimmicks in my lifetime, but this one is way over the top," Shay said as she stared out her window.

"No sooner than Jill had Sally set up and secured, Dale called her on Facetime. She made sure she held the phone away from her face so he could get a good look at their surroundings and chirped, "Hi, Dad."

"Hey, baby...are you at a fisherman's wharf?"

"No," Jill replied with a laugh and flipped the camera around, so Dale could get the full effect.

"Jill, where the hell are you?"

"Dad, words won't do it justice, but you're looking at a Bigfoot hunting camp in Tennessee. This is your mother's idea of a good time. Tonight at ten, we will go deep into the woods on an expedition."

"If you let Sally get shot, I will never forgive you."

Jill switched the camera around so it was on her face. "Thanks for your concern over my well-being."

"You know what I mean. None of you belong in a hunting camp. Jill, you're supposed to be in charge. I'm counting on you to make wise decisions, and this is not smart. Tell your grandmother that y'all need to find a more suitable and safer place. Do it now."

Jill grinned as Ella headed her way. "You tell her, Dad."

Ella took her phone from Jill and smiled. "Tell me what, honey?"

"Hi, Mom. Are you having a good time?"

"Wonderful, just lovely, especially since Anne and I came up with a new plan. You know, just about anyone can say they've been to the beach, but how many can say they've gone on a real Bigfoot hunt?" Ella's eyes sparkled as she said, "We're thinking about visiting an area where they say they see a lot of UFOs next. Doesn't that sound surreal?"

"It sounds…like something, Mom." Dale cleared his throat. "I don't think I'm very comfortable with y'all being at a hunting camp."

"It's not that kind of place, we hunt with cameras. I mean, there are guns, the staff here carry them for protection in case Bigfoot turns out to be unfriendly. So you see, we're very safe. Jill is taking very good care of us and Sally, too. You don't have to worry."

"Momma, you don't believe in Bigfoot. What're you doing out there?"

Ella held the phone close to her face, and once again, Dale saw nothing but nostrils and a pair of lipstick-covered lips. "Don't rain on my whimsy parade, Dale," she whispered.

"Okay, Mom, it's good to see you. Would you put Jill back on?"

"Yes, dear, love you." Ella handed the phone back to Jill.

"You're letting my momma go into the woods in the middle of the night to hunt a mythical creature," Dale said with a stern look.

"You've known her all your life. Ella Savoy does what she wants," Jill said, matching his expression. "I didn't hear you put your big ol' foot down."

"You just remember, if anything happens to them or Sally, it's on your head."

"You know what I've got on my head and shoulders right now? Your big-ass Sally and three women with their own ideas and wills, not to mention all the work I have piling up at the office. That makes me pretty damn badass, so give me a break."

"You're a younger version of your grandmother, hard-headed, cocky, bullish, and—"

Ella stuck her face in front of the camera. "You know I'm still standing here, right?"

"Hi, Mom."

"Please go on," Ella said sweetly.

"I…really need to get back to work. Love y'all, be careful," Dale said before his face disappeared from the screen.

Ella held up her fist, and Jill bumped it.

67

Chapter 9

Jill lifted her cowboy hat from her face when she heard movement near her hammock. Shay settled into one of the chairs beneath the awning with a book. They were all supposed to be napping in preparation for the big hunt.

"Can't sleep, either, huh?"

Shay gazed up at Jill. "I think it's the stew that Anne put on to slow cook. I'm not hungry, but all I can think about is eating it."

"She makes a good one." Jill laid her hat on her stomach and pointed at the netting above. "Does this place kinda make you wish you were back in Utah now?"

Shay smiled. "No."

"Is that where you're originally from?"

"You really don't know anything about me, do you?"

Jill started ticking off fingers as she spoke. "You're from Utah, you're a nurse and you don't like being one, a lesbian, you're not afraid of snakes, you like licorice. That's all I've got. I don't even know your last name."

"Macaluso. I was born in Baton Rouge and grew up there. I went to LSU, graduated, and with a need to assert my independence, I moved to Utah with some friends where I spent fourteen years."

"That makes you in your mid-thirties."

"I'm thirty-six."

Jill grinned. "I was gonna say you don't look a day over thirty-nine."

"I assume you're in your mid- to late forties."

Jill's grin vaporized. "I just turned forty."

"Eww, the F word." Shay pretended to shiver. "Hey, what does one wear to a Bigfoot hunt?"

"I'm wearing jeans and a hoodie, no underwear, though. If we come up on a bear and I wet my pants, that's just less I have to wash if I survive."

"Yeah, one pair of underwear can really make or break a load," Shay said with a laugh.

Jill climbed out of the hammock and joined Shay at the table. "What're you reading?"

Shay scooted the book closer to Jill. "It belongs to Anne, and it's all about vitamins. If you need to go to sleep, this is what you read."

"I'd prefer you just hit me over the head with it." Jill gazed at the simple silver cuff band around Shay's wrist. "I like your bracelet."

"Do you want it?"

Jill laughed. "If I say I like your car, will you give that to me too?"

"No, I'm still paying for it." Shay toyed with the band. "My ex gave me this. I need to take it off, and it's just going to sit in a box with the other things she refused to take back."

"Hmm." Jill rested her chin in her hand. "She didn't want to let you go, did she?"

Shay continued to stare at the bracelet and shook her head. "No, she wanted to work everything out, but I was too far gone."

"And you feel terribly guilty."

Shay exhaled heavily. "I've never been in her shoes."

"Are you telling me that no one has ever broken up with you?" Jill said with an incredulous tone.

"I've been dumped plenty of times, but I've never lost complete control. I've been pissed, and I threw away pictures and cards, spent a day eating ice cream, and moved on. I've never drunk myself stupid, though, or just…went crazy." Shay met Jill's gaze. "What's wrong with me?"

"Well, I think most people would say you have a lot of self-control. You weren't in love with her, were you?"

"I thought I was—could've been a little at the beginning." Shay traced the bracelet with her fingertip. "I always thought falling in love would be different, not so cerebral, but more of something I couldn't control. You said you fell hard for Jeri, what was it like?"

"Like being in a trance. I had a big group of friends, and one of them was dating Jeri, that's how I met her. I went to school at UNO, and Biloxi isn't that far from New Orleans, so we'd go to the beach every weekend and bake in the sun. Jeri and I would always gravitate to each other. We'd sit and talk while everyone else played volleyball or passed out from drinking the jungle juice we made with cheap liquor." Jill laughed. "Everyone would be scattered all over the beach drunk out of their skulls, and Jeri and I would gather them up and drive back to New Orleans. I would've been one of those pickled raisins, but I just wanted to hear everything she had to say. We could talk all day and never run out of interesting topics, and I became so entranced. She was all I could think about when we were apart, and I lived for the times I knew I'd pass her on campus." Jill shook her head. "I couldn't control my feelings, and I lost a friend because I stole Jeri from her."

"No...I've never been to that place," Shay said and unclipped the bracelet and let it fall to the table.

"That doesn't mean you won't find it. Just don't look for it at Paul's Bigfoot Safari."

Shay did her best to maintain a straight face as their hunting guide gave his speech. He was dressed in black from head to toe, and he'd painted his face and neck to match. She wondered what he thought of his crew and their apparel. Anne had on a pair of jogging pants with reflective stripes and a sweatshirt. Ella wore jeans and a yellow sweater. Shay took a cue from Jill and put on a pair of jeans and a dark blue Windbreaker over a long-sleeved T-shirt.

"Again, my name is Royce, and at this time, I ask you to turn off your phones or put them in airplane mode. It's imperative that you remain quiet if you have any hopes of seeing this legendary creature. Any questions?"

70

Jill raised her hand. "How many people have seen it?"

Royce pointed to a wall of pictures behind him.

Jill looked to be on the verge of losing her composure too, and asked, "Okay, then how come no one can focus properly? All those shots are blurry."

"Ma'am, it's a stunning thing. Even though people are prepared to photograph the Sasquatch, when that moment happens, they get a little excited. Some people run, and that's why we've begun doing our expeditions with all-terrain vehicles. We've had a lot of folks get lost out there. That's why I must remind you to stay in the vehicle at all times."

Ella raised her hand. "What if I have to go to the bathroom?"

"There are restroom stations throughout the perimeter," Royce replied a tad impatiently. "Now if you're ready, ladies, we need to go."

The group followed Royce outside single file. "So this is a mule?" Anne asked.

"It's actually a John Deere. We made modifications to make our guests comfortable and painted it black to blend in with the night." Royce handed everyone a pair of goggles. "These are infrared, they'll allow you to see in the dark. You can wear them over glasses, but you may need to adjust the strap for a comfortable fit."

Anne was the first to complain. "This is going to totally mess up my hair."

"We'll find a beauty shop," Ella said as she strapped hers on, making herself look like a redheaded bug, then she helped Anne with hers.

Jill put on her goggles and posed for a quick picture, then took one of Shay, Ella, and Anne. "Y'all are kind of greenish. Anne, for you, it's really working."

"Ladies, I must remind you that this is not a time for horseplay or jokes. You need to remain focused." Royce slipped on a helmet and adjusted the mic in front of his mouth. He slipped his goggles into place and gestured for everyone to climb into the vehicle.

Anne and Ella climbed into the front seat with Royce, leaving Shay and Jill to sit in the back. Jill had her hand over her

71

mouth and was shaking with silent laughter. "What is it?" Shay whispered.

Jill shook her head and waved her off. "I'm good," she said much higher than she normally spoke.

No one said a word as Royce drove the vehicle into the dark woods. Every so often, Jill would squeak, then inhale deeply. The light from the crescent moon above was almost completely shut out by the tree canopy. Shay jumped when she felt Jill's breath against her ear.

"This is the dumbest thing I've ever done, and he's so into this I can't stop laughing at him," Jill whispered.

Shay was teetering on the edge of hysterical laughter, and Jill wasn't helping. She pressed her hands to her mouth, breathed in deeply through her nose, and tried to imagine what it felt like to be hit by a stun gun.

"The woods can play tricks on your sight at night," Royce said softly. "A strong odor usually accompanies the Sasquatch, so if you smell something strange, pay very close attention."

"No, that would probably be Anne," Jill said, sounding like she'd inhaled helium.

Shay cackled. "I was gonna say that. I swear I was."

The cart stopped, and Royce sat still and silent because even Ella was chortling. When everyone calmed down, he said, "Ladies, if you want a chance to see the Sasquatch, you have to be absolutely quiet."

"We will," Ella assured him.

Just as the vehicle began to move again, a flash of light nearly blinded them all. Jill jerked her phone from the pocket of her sweatshirt and whispered. "I'm so sorry, but I have to take this just for a second."

"Jillian," Ella snapped. "You heard the rules."

"Hey," Jill said quickly and softly. "I can't talk right now, I'm hunting Bigfoot."

Selene's voice was so loud everyone could hear her as though she were on speaker. "Right," she said with a laugh.

"No, I'm serious, we're at a...I don't know what you would call it, but I'm in a mule thing wearing night-vision goggles. No shit."

Ella reached over the seat and swatted blindly. "Hang up that phone."

"I'll have to call you tomorrow. I'm so sorry," Jill whispered.

"Are you serious?" Selene asked incredulously.

The cart stopped abruptly, and Royce said, "Ma'am, I'm going to have to ask you to end that call, or the expedition is over."

"Is that a man?" Selene asked.

"Yes, and he's serious, and he has a gun. I have to go," Jill said.

"A fucking gun—what?" Selene practically yelled.

Anne had gotten out of the cart and snatched the phone from Jill. "She's not joking, and you have some mouth on you." Anne ended the call and switched the phone off before she stuck it in her pocket.

"I can't believe you just did that," Jill said completely stunned.

"Believe it, Jillian," Ella said firmly. "Now you're ruining this for the rest of us. Be quiet."

Shay waited for Royce to take off again and whispered against Jill's ear, "Was that your girlfriend?"

"I think *was* is the operative word in that question," Jill said softly.

Shay and Jill leaned in to say something at the same time, and their lips brushed. Shay snorted with laughter when she recoiled, and Jill did the same. The cart came to an abrupt stop again.

"Sir, I am so sorry." Ella patted him on the arm. "We're all a little nervous and scared, and we get a little giddy when we're that way."

"I am absolutely petrified," Jill managed to say before she completely dissolved into tears and laughter.

"Listen…listen!" Royce rasped.

Jill was against Shay's shoulder laughing and doing her best to muffle it, but Shay did hear something in the distance, and it sounded big. Jill quieted and sat up. The woods fell completely silent.

73

"That could be a bear," Shay whispered.

"All right, that's not funny," Jill said just as softly. "I saw some pictures of a hiker that got mauled."

"You are safe with me," Royce said firmly.

Their guide looked as though he might've weighed a hundred fifty pounds, and he was strapped with a stun gun. Shay had very little faith in his abilities to fend off a raccoon, much less a bear. She leaned forward and asked him, "How fast will this cart go?"

"Ma'am, I assure you that this vehicle will get us out of here if we need to make a fast retreat. Do you smell that?"

"That was me, I call it." Ella raised a hand. "I'm scared shitless."

"Ladies, if you will look to the west, just half a click on that rise—"

"What the fuck is a click?" Jill half-shouted. "Are we close to a bear?"

"Jillian!"

"Ma'am, I am a professional. I have tracked animals since I was a boy, and I can tell you with one hundred percent certainty that is a Sasquatch on that rise, and it is slowly moving toward us. Get your cameras ready, remain calm, and be quiet."

Jill leaned close to Shay and whispered, "He keeps calling me ma'am."

Shay didn't see anything on the rise, but she could hear something moving in on them very slowly. She raised her phone with her thumb poised above the shutter button. Anne had an actual camera, and she was steadily snapping pictures in the direction of the noise.

"I have an issue with bears, it started right after I saw those photos on the Web," Jill admitted seriously. "I have to tell y'all that I am not comfortable with sitting here waiting for one of them to come up and pick me out of this cart like a nacho."

"Quiet, I think I have him," Anne breathed out.

Shay didn't see what Anne did, but as the crackling of the underbrush grew louder, she inadvertently pressed the shutter on her phone. The flash seemed to stay on indefinitely, and the shutter made the sound it did when it was being held. In a matter of seconds, she'd blinded them all and had taken dozens of shots.

"He ran right in front of me," Ella exclaimed. "It was so close I could've touched its fur."

Jill sucked her teeth and stood with her hands on her hips as she stared at each picture Shay swiped in front of her. "So Bigfoot wears combat boots. No wonder we don't find many tracks."

Anne and Ella tried to hide the fact they were laughing behind their bedtime snack cookies. Anne raised her glass of milk and said, "Three hundred and twenty bucks well spent."

"On what?" Shay asked, wide-eyed.

"We shelled out eighty dollars a ticket for that adventure," Ella said with a smile. "And I would say we got our money's worth."

Jill threw a hand up. "Tomorrow, I'm going to that office to demand a refund with those pictures Shay took. This is a rip-off and a tourist trap."

Ella and Anne exchanged glances and rolled with laughter. "We saw Bigfoot. That's what we paid for," Ella said.

"We're missing something here, Jill." Shay folded her arms and stared at the giggling pair. "Out with it."

"Had y'all done more than turn your noses up at the website, you would've read the line that said, 'Guaranteed Bigfoot sighting.' Of course, it's a hoax." Anne snorted. "What makes it so funny is how you two acted so childish, then totally freaked out there at the end."

"For the record, I was calm," Shay said indignantly.

"Y'all let me think we were gonna be eaten by bears." Jill nodded. "Okay...all right."

"I think we're about to be threatened with payback," Ella said with a smile.

Jill waved her off. "Nah. I'm just pacing around adjusting to the fact a little pee came out of me back there for nothing."

"Serves you right for being so rude for taking that call," Ella said disapprovingly.

"I was supposed to call Selene and forgot. And hey, Anne, thank you ever so much for chastising her." Jill scowled. "I hope you're noting the sarcasm."

"I don't like the foul-mouthed hussy already," Anne said defiantly.

"You are just as foul," Jill argued. "Granted, you don't drop the F-bomb."

"You did," Anne retorted.

"I was under duress."

"Which one of you is going to take a shower first?" Ella asked after a yawn.

"Shay, you go." Jill pulled her phone from her pocket. "I have to send Dad a text to let him know we survived, then I need to email Selene and apologize. I can't text her this late and run the chance of waking her up."

"Yes, I'm sure she's one of those women who need a lot of beauty sleep," Ella quipped.

"You should probably let us check you for ticks first," Anne said to Shay. "You don't want Lyme disease."

Shay grabbed her bag and moved quickly toward the bathroom. "That's all right, I'm sure I can do it myself."

"Now that's a nice woman," Anne said softly with her gaze fixed on Jill, who was tapping on the screen of her phone. "You'd be lucky to find someone like that."

"You can stop right there," Jill said while she continued to type.

"Let me take a stab at what this Selene is like." Anne ticked off fingers as she spoke. "She's probably kind of bitchy. She wears expensive clothes and puts way too much makeup on her face. She's probably some big to-do at her job or wants to be."

"Jeri wasn't like that at all, aside from ambition. She was a down-to-earth woman. Since that relationship ended, you've been dating nothing but women who—I'm sorry, but they're overdressed...bitches." Ella held up a hand. "There, I said it."

Jill continued to stare at her phone. "That is so...backward. You're saying if a woman is strong, then she's a bitch. Both of you are strong women, and you raised me to be the same. Don't you see how hypocritical that is?"

"No, honey, strong is a virtue. It's the holier-than-thou attitude I despise, and every woman you've been involved with since Jeri is like that. Have you ever stopped to consider that might be why you haven't been happy with any of them?" Ella sighed. "Baby, I think you're getting arrogance confused with strength."

"Selene isn't like that," Jill said firmly.

Ella grew impatient. "Do you really know that? You said you've only gone on a couple of dates with her."

"So I'll have to go on a few more with her to find out." Jill set her phone aside and gave Ella her full attention. "That's how dating works. Why are we having this discussion right now? It's because you'd rather me pursue Shay," Jill said with a nod. "You picked her out for me. As I recall the story, your parents had already chosen the perfect man for you, and you ran off with Grandpa John."

"I knew John was right for me the minute I met him, and I was right," Ella argued. "That's a gift we Savoy women have, we're very discerning. That's why I'm so stunned that you're ignoring yours. Jillian, you know the women you've been seeing aren't what you need. If I'm to be truly frank, I think it's because you're afraid of getting hurt again, which is understandable the way Jeri left you, but—"

"She didn't leave me, it was a mutual understanding," Jill said coolly. "We tried the long-distance thing, and it didn't work out."

Ella gazed at her sadly. "Because in less than one month, she was seeing someone else. Baby, you said it once in a moment of complete devastation, Jeri left you before she moved from Baton Rouge."

"It's late," Anne began as she regarded the tormented expression on Jill's face. "This is a topic for another time."

Ella forged on. "I don't want to say or do anything to hurt you, but I can't continue to allow you to lie to yourself anymore."

"Anne is right, this isn't the time." Jill got up and headed for the door. "Y'all go ahead and shower when Shay gets out. I'm gonna take a walk."

77

Shay was already in bed when Jill came back in. She wasn't expecting the cold hard look Jill gave her for a second before she grabbed her things and continued on to the bathroom. Anne and Ella seemed at odds with each other after Shay got out of the shower, and she wondered if perhaps the three of them had gotten into an argument.

She left her earplugs out and tried to read Anne's book about vitamins until Jill finished in the bathroom in case she wanted to talk. When Jill emerged from her shower, she climbed into bed wordlessly and switched off the light above it. Shay glanced at Jill every so often and noticed that she was staring at the ceiling with her arms tucked behind her head.

"Is my light bothering you?" Shay asked.

"No."

"Is something wrong?"

Jill took so long to answer that Shay thought she'd been ignored. Finally, Jill said, "No."

"Do you want to talk? You listened to me today, and I'm willing to return the favor."

"Not tonight, Shay, but thanks."

Chapter 10

No one stirred until almost nine the next morning. Jill got up first and made coffee with the previous night's conversation with Ella still fresh in her mind. She trusted her grandmother to always tell her the truth, but Jill wasn't entirely sure Ella was right this time. Ella's case did have some merit, though. Jill could never truly accept that somewhere along the way Jeri had fallen out of love with her. She'd preferred to cling to the story that she'd told Shay—their eventual breakup was mutual. The truth was that Jill would've moved to New Mexico, but six months before they were to leave, Jeri told Jill she wanted to go alone and used the excuse she couldn't take Jill from her family.

It was also true that every relationship Jill had since Jeri was short-lived. She dated with high hopes, but Jill never felt that mind- and heart-blowing rush she'd felt with Jeri, no matter how she longed for it. She wondered if Ella had hit the proverbial nail on the head. Maybe she truly was subconsciously seeking out the wrong women.

That line of thinking made her think hard about Selene. Jill was physically attracted to her, and they talked easily, but in truth, they had very little in common. Jill learned on the first date that Selene was very interested in politics. She worked for the state in a division that investigated fraud. Selene's office specialized in insurance fraud, and Selene had expressed a desire to one day run for insurance commissioner. Jill was about as interested in politics as she was foot fungus. Selene's idea of a good time was a spirited debate with someone who had opposing views. Selene had told Jill that she and friends routinely got together over drinks to discuss political issues. She referred to it as "verbal tennis." Jill preferred to play the game with a racket and a ball. Still, Jill held to the adage that opposites attract, but the more she thought, the more merit Ella's theory gained. Jill could never see herself enjoying a night out with Selene's friends, and she doubted they'd think much of her.

"What time is it?" Shay whispered as she sat up in bed.

"Nine," Jill said without trying to temper the volume of her voice.

"If you're out there flapping your gums, I hope you're brewing the coffee," Anne hollered from the bedroom.

The door opened, and Ella plodded into the kitchen area looking bleary-eyed. "What time did we go to bed?"

Jill shrugged. "Sometime after one."

"Well, ladies, it's cereal or oatmeal or whatever you can find in the fridge for breakfast." Ella scratched her head with a yawn. "I'm too tired to cook."

Anne came out of their room wearing a yellow cotton robe, her Napoleon hat hairdo listing to the port side. "I'll tell you what, I feel like I've been beaten."

"You look like it too," Jill quipped with a grin.

Anne patted her on the cheek roughly. "I love you, you little shit. What's on the agenda for today?"

"This place has a two-night stay minimum, but I say we leave the money on the table and hit the road." Ella poured cream into her cup. "I don't like it here, it's too oppressive with all the tarps and netting. We're not far from Virginia and that campground that claims to have a lot of UFO activity."

Jill gazed at her with a grin. "Is there a green man guarantee?"

Ella ignored her and turned to Shay. "Honey, do you have any requests?"

Shay shook her head. "I'm just along for the ride."

"Well, you speak up if there's something you want to do," Anne added.

"All right, so we're getting out of here today." Jill looked at her watch. "Can we all be ready for noon?" Everyone nodded in agreement. "Good, I'm taking my coffee outside, no one bother me."

Then everyone followed her outside.

To Jill's utter dismay, the woman Ella spoke with when she made the reservations at the next campground told her about a beauty shop close by. Ella promptly made appointments. The high side for Jill was a sporting goods store in the same shopping center as the salon.

"Text me when y'all are done, and we'll meet up," Jill said with a glance at her watch.

"Shay, you're coming with us." Ella took her by the hand. "Jill will have you combing every aisle of that boring store if you don't."

"But I like—okay," Shay said as Ella half-dragged her through the parking lot.

Jill thought to object because Shay didn't look thrilled with the invitation, but she needed some time alone. She headed across the parking lot toward the store and looked over her shoulder just as Ella and Anne led Shay into the salon. A wave of empathy surged through Jill, and she changed her course, then stopped. For all she knew, Shay might've loved beauty shops.

"You're a grown woman, Shay. If you don't want to be in there, just say no." Jill waited a moment, and when Shay didn't come out, she continued on.

She pulled her phone from her pocket unwilling to disturb Selene at work with a call, but she did send a text. *In case you haven't read my email yet, I'm very sorry about what happened last night. The hunt threw me off schedule, and I forgot to call. I want to apologize for Anne hanging up on you, as well.*

Jill tucked the phone into her pocket and went inside the sporting goods store. First, she went through the clothing section to see if there was anything she couldn't live without, then on to the fishing gear. Jill had only brought along one rod and reel, and she looked at them with Shay in mind. She wondered if perhaps Shay would enjoy fishing with her. The purchase seemed like a waste, though, since Shay had talked about leaving, and Jill realized then she found that disappointing.

She had less than a couple of seconds to ponder her feelings when her phone rang and Selene's name appeared on the ID. "Hey," Jill said with a smile when she answered.

"I've only got a few minutes between meetings. Are you really serious? Did you hunt for Bigfoot last night?" Selene asked in a whisper.

"It wasn't my idea. The last thing I wanted to do was wander the Tennessee hills in search of a mythical creature. Look, I'm sorry."

"Yes, you said that in your text, I understand."

Jill stuffed a hand in her pocket and said, "Can I ask you something?"

"Sure, but make it quick."

"Does it bother you that I'm not into politics?"

"Wow, that was random," Selene said with a laugh. "I haven't given it much thought to tell you the truth. Why do you ask?"

"I was just wondering if that would cause a problem down the road."

"Jill, honey, we're still standing on the corner. Let's keep this casual, okay? One date at a time."

"I obviously have too much time on my hands to think right now," Jill said with a weak laugh. "I just…I was wondering."

"I have to go now, my assistant is waving me into the meeting. Call me later."

The call ended, and Jill slipped the phone back into her pocket and all thoughts of Selene along with it. She looked at the rod and reel again and pulled it down from the display.

Ella had sent the text that they were done, but as Jill crossed the parking lot, she didn't see them near Sally, and they weren't outside the salon. That suited Jill just fine; she was able to tuck her gift away and would give it to Shay later when they were alone. She was walking toward the beauty shop when Shay came out the door moving fast. The first thing Jill noticed was Shay's hair and how it appeared really big. As Shay drew closer, Jill realized she looked like she was wearing a mask with big blue streaks over the eyes and giant red pouty lips.

"What happened to you?" Jill asked in shock.

"I'm not sure," Shay said, looking just as stunned. "One minute, I was reading a magazine, and the next, two women that looked like Dolly Parton descended on me like vultures. They started putting stuff on my face, then they did all kinds of things to my hair."

Anne walked out of the shop next; her Napoleon hat 'do rode higher than ever. Ella followed with her little red hair ball reinflated. "Doesn't Shay just look beautiful?" Ella chirped.

She looked like a hooker who'd just survived a wind tunnel, but Jill nodded and tried to smile.

Anne looked pleased when she said, "We treated her to a surprise makeover."

"It worked, she looks very surprised," Jill said, feeling truly sorry for Shay. She didn't wear makeup, but the women she knew who did had said blue eyeshadow was a big no-no. Shay had it up to her brows, and they looked like they had been painted and shaped into two very thick rectangular boxes. It was horrifying.

"I'm starved. Why don't we go eat somewhere instead of cooking tonight?" Anne suggested.

Ella patted her on the shoulder. "Excellent idea, dear. There's a steakhouse right over there. We could walk to it instead of having to get Sally back on the road."

Shay blinked rapidly, and Jill didn't know if it was because the huge fake eyelashes were heavy or if she was mortified about being seen like that by other people. "Your eyes look really bloodshot," Jill said. "I think whatever they put on you is causing a reaction. Pretty as you look, you should consider going straight to the bathroom and washing your face when we get to the restaurant."

"I think you're right," Shay agreed and started to run a hand through her hair before she remembered it was sprayed with enough hairspray to withstand a hurricane. "I'm very sorry that I'm going to ruin your present, ladies."

"Oh, honey, that's okay, we don't want you to be uncomfortable." Ella shoved a bag at her. "Besides, we bought you more eyelashes, mascara, shadows, and liner, and it's all supposed to be hypoallergenic. It's so nice to have another girly girl to do things like this with. We can't even get Jill to walk past a makeup counter."

"That's…very sweet of you both, thank you," Shay said as she took the bag.

"Let's get to hiking, I may pass out from starvation before we get there," Anne said and strode off with Ella right behind her.

Jill walked slowly, allowing them to get a lead, and smiled at Shay, who strolled beside her. "Shay…you have got to learn to say no—hell no."

"I'm not on that comfort level with them yet, and they thought they were doing something nice," Shay said miserably. "I could only glance in the mirror for a second. Do I look as bad as I think I do? Just give it to me straight."

"You look like a nineteen fifties cocktail waitress with a wig on."

Shay released a heavy sigh. "Oh, my God."

"Can I take your pic—?"

"No."

Jill patted Shay on the back. "We're gonna laugh at this later, take heart."

"It's gonna be a long time."

As they walked into the restaurant, Shay went straight to the restroom. Jill went to the table with Ella and Anne so she would know where they would be seated. "I'm gonna go to the bathroom, and I'll let Shay know where our table is at," Jill said, instead of sitting down.

"Honey, take her these." Ella pulled a packet from her purse. "They're my emergency makeup removal towelettes. They'll get more of the makeup off her eyes than soap and water, and they're less irritating."

Jill took the packet and found the bathroom. Shay had a wad of toilet paper and was scrubbing at her face with it. The fragile tissue left behind chunks on her eyelids.

"Grandma says use these." Jill opened the packet. "Let me help you." She took Shay's chin in her hand and started with the garish eyebrows first. "I see you got the lashes off. They look like two dead caterpillars in the sink."

Shay groaned. "That was kind of painful because they took some of my real ones."

"I noticed they have a lot of drink specials here. You should order one or ten, it might make you feel better. No, don't laugh, it causes your eyes to crease. Do you want to keep the lipstick?"

"No, that's irritating my eyes too."

Jill laughed. "Keep them closed, I'm still working here."

"Thank you for bringing me the makeup removers. I thought I was going to have to hide in here until y'all finished eating."

Jill took out another towelette and wiped Shay's lips with it. "I've got your back. May I touch your hair?"

"Not too hard, I'm afraid it'll break off."

Jill very carefully placed a hand on Shay's high standing 'do. She bit her lip to keep from laughing. "Oh, I have an idea." Jill took her sunglasses from where they hung on the neck of her T-shirt and very carefully set them atop Shay's head, then lost all composure. "I thought they would weigh it down, but they're just riding up there."

Shay turned and looked at herself in the mirror. Jill had done a good job of removing the makeup, but her hair was a completely different story. The so-called hairdressers had teased and sprayed the top of her hair so much that it looked like a giant squid wearing sunglasses, and the sides of her hair were its legs. She blew out a heavy sigh.

Jill stood beside Shay and dropped a hand on her shoulder. "I really would like to take—"

"No pictures."

"I usually prefer state parks, they're most often much nicer, but, Grandma, this is pretty awesome," Jill said with her hands on her hips.

Vegetation had been allowed to grow around each campsite and made somewhat of a wall between them. The campground was built around a lake and bisected by streams and hiking trails. Though it was very close to a town, Jill still felt like they were in the wilderness. She couldn't wait to explore it all.

"I booked us here for a few days," Ella said. "Anne and I are losing steam. We're gonna need a day or two to just relax and recharge. I hope you and Shay won't be too bored. Y'all can always take the scooter and go into town. I noticed it had a movie theater."

"Yeah, we might do a few things if she decides to stay."

Ella's brow rose as she regarded Jill. "She said she would."

"For a few days, but she's not sold on the idea of making the whole trip."

Ella grimaced and shook her head. "Anne told me she had Shay convinced to stay, and I rubbed her feet after the Sasquatch hunt. She played me like a cheap fiddle. I used lotion, Jill. It was a committed rub."

"Now I'll tell you what, if you don't wash your hair for a few days and wrap it like I do mine with a paper towel band, it'll stay just like that," Anne said as she followed Shay to where Jill and Ella were standing.

Anne inhaled sharply and looked out across the small canyon behind their campsite. "I do not want to roll off into that. Jill, did you do a good job of chocking the wheels?"

"This plateau is as flat as a board, but yes, everything is secure," Jill said as she gazed at Shay. "Do you want to do a little exploring before it gets dark?"

Shay nodded. "I'm game."

"Hook up the satellite before you go, monkey. I want to watch some TV," Anne said. "I need to see the weather and what's been happening in the world."

After Anne and Ella were happily tucked in watching the news, Jill and Shay hit the trails. Jill glanced at Shay and said, "I remember you saying you weren't into hiking much, so we won't go very far."

"I would classify this as a walk, and I'm enjoying it." Shay released a happy sigh. "This really is a pretty place. Hey, did you patch things up with Selena?"

"Selene," Jill corrected. "Yeah, she's not angry with me."

Shay nodded. "That's good."

Neither of them said anything as they strolled lazily along the road that wound through the campground. Shay had decided that she really liked Jill. She put on a good tough front, but underneath, she was kind and sensitive. Shay felt a tiny sliver of envy for Selene.

"What's your greatest fear?" Jill asked out of the blue.

"I think I just lived it in that salon."

Jill's laugh seemed to echo off the rock wall beside the road.

"Seriously."

"I've already mentioned public speaking. A completely closed mind, I suppose. My brother fascinates and scares me at the same time. I don't know what happened to Clark. We were close growing up, but then he married Leann, and she and her family are super religious. Clark and I didn't always agree, but at least we respected each other's views, and that all changed. He told me that he could not condone my lifestyle, as if he had a right. The word lifestyle really rankled me. That implies choice, and I am so sick of hearing that bullshit doctrine. I didn't choose my eye color, and I did not choose to be a lesbian, that is what I am. What really scares me, though, is that I'm so angry about his view of me that I made my own judgments of him and everyone that darkens the doorstep of a church. I worry that I have become just as narrow-minded and judgmental as he is. It's hard for me to adopt the live and let live attitude for him and his kind."

"It's a tightrope. I struggle with it too. I hired a woman to work with me, and she was excellent at her job, always on time, courteous, and very thorough. I have no doubt she knew I was a lesbian when she first met me at the interview. One day, she drove into the parking lot with a brand-new bumper sticker on her car, and it said something like, 'God Didn't Create Adam and Steve.' She never voiced her views in the office, but that sticker spoke volumes. It was so offensive to me, and I was so mad I wanted to fire her just to get her and her bumper sticker out of my face. But then, I had to consider that I would be doing something I absolutely despised, which is discriminating. I took the high road, and I treated her fairly."

"Does she still work for you?"

"No, she resigned when her husband was transferred out of state, but I gave her a going-away party and a bonus like I did for anyone else whose work is exemplary. Maybe by putting that sticker on her car, she felt she could influence me, maybe it was to provoke. Either way, I know I made an impact on her even if she'll never acknowledge it. Despite our differing view, I didn't disparage, degrade, or treat her with disrespect, and maybe she'll *choose* to do that for someone else she doesn't agree with."

Shay smiled. "You sound like a good boss."

Jill laughed again. "There are two women that work with me in accounting, and one of them has been there for six years. Karen and I have a good working relationship. The other has been there a year, and I want to choke her on a daily basis. Gwen will screw something up and lie about it rather than admitting she made a mistake. She is a true test of the sensitivity training I went through."

"You had to be trained...to be sensitive?"

Jill nodded. "I've fired countless people, and I've absolutely lost my mind on some of them. My mother sat me down one day after I'd berated an employee until he cried. After she explained to me that I was the one with the issues, I elected to take a class on management and dealing with staff. In my family, if we have a problem, we just yell at each other or make sarcastic comments, but you can't manage people like that, not successfully anyway."

"I like your sarcasm."

Jill smiled. "I enjoy yours too."

"So what's your greatest fear? Don't say bears because I really don't think you'd be out here walking with me if it was."

"Asparagus."

Shay laughed. "Seriously."

Jill thought for a moment. "Being wrong. Most days, I think I know myself pretty well, then I get thrown a curve ball, and it makes me question all my motives. I just don't want to be old and look back on my life and say, 'Wow, I really screwed that up.'"

"We don't live a life without regret. We're human, and invariably, we're going to mess up a lot of things. You know that, right?"

"Alone," Jill blurted out. "I don't want to grow old alone." She stopped walking, bent at the waist, and put her hands on her knees. "I didn't realize how much that bothered me until I said it."

Shay tentatively laid a hand on Jill's back. "I think we all fear that."

Jill stood up straight and started walking fast. "I cannot believe I just admitted that to you."

"Why not?" Shay said as she caught up with her. "We don't know each other. That's why it was so easy for me to tell you that I've never fallen in love. I'm thirty-six, and I'm like a love virgin. I've got the Tin Man disease, and at the rate I'm going, I may rust before I get a heart."

"You have one, and you use it. You did allow Grandma and Anne to drag you into a salon where two Dolly Parton clones gave you a beehive and a Halloween facial."

Shay clutched her hair with both hands. "Oh, dear God, I forgot I had this on my head." She veered off the paved road onto a trail marked: *Squatter's Creek*.

"Where are you going? Jill asked as she followed.

"Swimming."

"Did you miss the sign? You want to dive into something with squat in the name? I've got horrible mental images. I'll bet down the road the next sign reads *Turd River*."

"I think you're interpreting that incorrectly."

"Oh, man, up here in the mountains? That water is gonna be cold," Jill said with a laugh. "I'll bet you twenty bucks you won't so much as put a foot in it."

"You're gonna owe me thirty-four dollars, I deducted six for the licorice." Shay held up a finger. "That's a reminder that you haven't paid up on the last bet."

There was no sandy beach, but there was a big boulder that someone had spray painted: *Absolutely No Diving*. Shay scampered up onto it and placed her hands on her hips gathering her courage. Jill climbed up behind her and gazed at the water a few feet below.

"It's kinda chilly out here. Why do you want to swim?"

Shay threw a hand in the air. "Anne told me not to wash my hair, so it would stay like this. I think they like it, so I'm gonna accidentally fall into the creek."

"Is your phone in your pocket?"

"No, I—Jill!" Shay's eyes were huge as she hung over the edge of the water. Jill had a firm grip on her forearms, and only one of Shay's feet remained on the rock. "This could be better, I can tell them you threw me in."

"True, and you don't have to make the decision to jump." Jill grinned. "See, I told you, I've got your back."

"I don't feel as grateful this time," Shay said with a nervous laugh.

"You hit the water and swim right out, then it's all done. You do know how to swim, don't you?"

"Since I was five."

"Okay, good. You have everything you need. I'm gonna let you go now," Jill said with a smile.

"No, don't warn me, talk for few minutes and drop me, but don't tell me when you're gonna do it."

"I bought you a fishing rod today in case you want to fish with me."

Shay looked even more surprised than when Jill grabbed and dangled her off the side of the boulder. "No kidding? I love to fish."

"Then go get one." Jill laughed as Shay made a huge splash, then she jumped in after her. The water was so cold, she felt like she was being stabbed by thousands of needles at once. When she broke the surface, Shay was already climbing onto the bank, screaming.

"Oh, my God, what was I thinking? Not worth it, so not worth it. I think my kidneys are frozen…Jill?"

Jill's teeth were chattering so hard, she couldn't speak. She crawled onto the rock-strewn shore and groaned. "Idea…so bad."

"Did you fall in?" Shay asked as she gave her a hand up.

90

"Jumped. Your hair…is still the same."

Shay's face fell until she put her hands on her head. "You are such a liar, that's why you shower second."

Jill watched Shay take off running and did her best to follow with water squishing out of her sneakers.

Chapter 11

"You ruined her hairdo, Jillian," Ella said as she made hot chocolate. "I can't believe you did that, it was so pretty. I wouldn't be surprised if both of you were sick by tomorrow morning."

Showered and somewhat thawed, Jill and Shay were tucked in their beds. They exchanged mischievous smiles when Ella's back was turned. Everyone could hear Anne in the back bathroom complaining about the lukewarm shower she was forced to take after they used up most of the hot water.

"What were you playing again?" Ella asked.

"Queen of the rock." Jill flashed a triumphant smile. "I won."

"Don't look so smug. One or both of you could've gotten hurt." Ella handed a cup to Shay. "Y'all aren't teenagers anymore."

"Well, let me ask you this, Grandma. If you and Anne had been standing on that boulder, and y'all were our age, would you have shoved her off?"

Ella pursed her lips as she handed Jill a cup. "No, she was always faster than me, and I knew the payback would be severe." She smiled at Shay. "You have to be sly with your pranks when you're smaller. I've put everything in her coffee from mustard to pickle relish."

Jill pointed at Ella. "That's who I get my wicked streak from."

"Speaking of, your father called on that Face thing while you were out playing in the creek," Ella said. "I told him that we moved on to Virginia because someone shot a taillight out of Sally at the hunting camp. You should've seen his face. He pitched a fit until Anne took my phone out to the back of the camper and proved it wasn't true."

"Ella, the shower's all yours, but prepare yourself for tepid water," Anne griped as she walked into the room in her robe. She glared at Jill and Shay. "Y'all are idiots, just so you know."

Jill raised her cup in salute. "Thanks for pointing that out."

"I'm skipping the shower tonight since I had one this morning," Ella announced. "Good night, ladies, and I use that term loosely."

Anne grabbed a handful of paper towels for a new headband. "I'm beating you both in the morning. I'm just too damn tired to do it tonight."

"Mission accomplished," Jill said softly with a laugh when the bedroom door closed behind Anne. "You're back to normal, and I like it."

Shay raised her cup again. "Thank you ever so much for your assistance. I could've just washed my hair and claimed that I forgot that I wasn't supposed to, but it was a little exhilarating to be thrown off that rock, at least until I hit the water." Shay shook her head. "I can't believe you jumped in."

"Hey, I told you, I've got your back. If you suffer, I suffer."

"Do you mind if I use your computer tomorrow?" Shay asked and noted how quickly Jill's smile faded.

"Sure, you can use it. Are you still considering renting a car?"

"No, I wanted to log into my account and check on the status of my RN license. I had to renew it, and when I did, the state kicked it back and said I wasn't in the system. I've been going back and forth with them for a month. I won't look at your porn site."

Jill's smile returned. "It's a good one, you may want to make a note of it in case you ever need to do that kind of shopping."

Shay's left eyebrow arched. "I'll keep that in mind."

"What's your guilty pleasure when you're at home?" Jill's eyes flashed open wide, and she laughed. "I shouldn't have

93

asked that question right after a comment about sex toys. I mean, what do you like to do?"

"I like to watch movies. On a lazy day, I'll rent a bunch and have a marathon."

"Grandma mentioned she saw a movie theater in town. You wanna take the scooter out tomorrow and see one?"

"Yeah, I'd love to."

"Okay, this is a biggie because this will determine whether or not we can be friends. What genre?"

Shay clutched her cup with both hands and smiled. "You guess."

"I'm gonna go with dramatic chick flicks."

Shay shook her head slowly. "Try again."

Jill's face went blank. "Documentaries," she said, trying to keep the derision from her tone.

"I like action, sci-fi, thrillers, and on occasion, romantic comedies."

"I'm seeing you in a whole new light," Jill said before taking a sip of her hot chocolate.

"How do you see me?" Shay asked, genuinely curious.

"A little distant around new people. You have your pride. You didn't want me to pay for the licorice, and you demanded to buy dinner tonight. You're sweet, and despite claiming you have no heart, I think you put the feelings of others before yours, maybe sometimes to a fault. You have a delicate feminine exterior that hides some butchiness. You did pick up a snake, and you kind of drove the scooter like a dirt bike. You're like a treasure hunt, a person has to gradually get to know you to find all the good stuff you keep hidden."

That answer was more than Shay expected. She sat in stunned silence for a moment, then finished her hot chocolate.

"Shit!" Jill tossed her blankets aside. "I forgot to call Selene, and I told her I would." With socks on her feet, she stepped into a pair of flip-flops and crept to the door. "Good night, Shay."

"Night." Shay got up and put her cup away and brushed her teeth. She left the light on above Jill's bed and switched off her own. As she burrowed back into the covers, she thought about all Jill had said and how it had touched her.

94

She wasn't sure if Chris had ever observed her that closely. Chris's aloof demeanor had been what drew Shay to her in the first place. Shay had just stopped seeing someone who was overly clingy and needy, and Chris was a refreshing change. It stunned Shay how fast she became enamored with Chris, until a subtle shift occurred in their relationship. She started making little quips about how Shay dressed, the food she ate, the shows she watched, and it seemed a lot like disapproval. Shay's self-preservation kicked in and covered her heart with armor. Shay was never sure if Chris saw her truly for who she was or what she wanted her to be.

Ella's phone chimed, and the screen lit up the room. "Is it lightning?" Anne asked groggily.

"I think I have a text." Ella sat up, put on her glasses, and stared at the screen. *I need to talk to you. Now.*

Startled, Ella climbed out of bed and threw on her robe. She walked out of the bedroom and gently closed the door behind her. Jill's bed was empty, and Shay sat up and gazed at her curiously.

"Did I wake you, sweetie?" Ella asked as she tied the belt to her robe.

"No, I was awake."

"Where's Jill?" Ella asked casually.

"She went outside to talk to Selene."

"I need to talk to her, I'm sorry to have disturbed you," Ella said and stepped outside.

"Over here," Jill whispered from the shadows.

"Child, what is going on? That text you sent lit up my phone like a Christmas tree and scared me half to death. Is it your stomach, do you need a laxative?"

"What? No...wait, do you have any?" Jill held up both hands. "Never mind. I'm having a moment, and I need your help. I'm ready to listen to you now."

"Listen to me do what?"

"I tried to call Selene, and I couldn't...I don't want to." Jill pointed toward the camper. "I think it's her fault."

"Sally's?"

95

"No! Why are you so slow on the uptake tonight?"

"I was sleeping so soundly I was an inch above death." Ella threw a hand on her hip. "You're just gonna have to speak plainly until I get all my faculties back."

"All right, I've been doing a lot of thinking about what you said last night. It really got under my skin and pissed me off," Jill said as she began to pace. "I hate to admit this, but I think I have to agree with you. I have been dating the wrong women."

Ella smiled. "Now I see."

"Don't gloat."

"I'm not, dear," Ella said but continued to smile.

"Okay, here's the problem. I think I like Shay, but I'm not sure if it's because you put that idea in my head. We're out in the woods, I'm out of my element, I'm not thinking clearly. I bought her a rod and reel. What does that mean?"

Ella shrugged. "I think that means you like her. And I have to disagree with you, honey. I think your mind is clearer than it has been in a while. Maybe it took you coming out here to really get in touch with yourself. Shay isn't the type of woman you've been dating, but maybe she's the kind you should hope to find."

Jill shoved her hands into her hair and groaned. "I'm so confused."

"Jillian, honey, don't take offense to what I'm about to say. We've all seen it, your mom and dad, Anne. You loved deeply, you got hurt. You're a genuine and sincere person, and that's what you need in a mate to be happy. The women you've been involved with might be right for someone else, but not for you." Ella took Jill's hand and squeezed it. "I'm getting to know Shay too, and from what I can tell, she has more substance in her little toe than the hags you've been dragging up."

"You started off so sweet, then you went right for the jugular."

"It's cold, and I've got a warm bed waiting on me. Granted, I have to share it with a gas bubble on legs, but I do want to get back in there sometime tonight. Spend some more time with Shay, find out who she is. It may work out that you two will only be friends, but you know for sure that floozy you've been

96

seeing will never be what you want, and she won't be your friend."

Jill nodded. "Okay."

Ella stood on her toes and kissed Jill's cheek. "It's time for bed."

Chapter 12

After breakfast the next morning, Shay sat at the table outside with Jill's computer. Jill watched her from the window, peeking at the screens Shay was looking at. She'd made up her mind if Shay pulled up a rental car site, she'd go out there and accidentally smash her computer.

"What're y'all gonna do today?" Jill asked Anne and Ella as they sat around in their pajamas with coffee and a book of crossword puzzles.

"This is it," Anne said behind a yawn. "I don't have the energy to frolic."

Ella's phone rang, and she handed it to Jill. "Your father is awake."

Jill pressed a button, and Dale's face filled the screen. "Well, there you are," he said with a smile. "See, Viv, she wasn't eaten by a bear."

Vivian's face appeared next to Dale's. "I saw some horrid pictures of a bear mauling on the Internet this morning. You know what, Jill, just stay out of the woods. Find a mall and hike in it. Are you having fun?"

"Yes, the thrills just keep coming," Jill deadpanned.

"You should be here," Viv said with a grin. "Your father has found a unique way to install the window you've always wanted in your office." Dale pursed his lips and looked away. Viv moved closer to the screen. "He backed into the wall with his truck, even with the fancy camera on the back. Your office is totally being renovated."

Jill's heart sank. "How bad is the damage?"

"Not bad," Dale said nonchalantly.

"If I would've done it, he'd be telling you how catastrophic it was right now," Vivian said with a roll of her eyes. "Let's put it this way, you're getting a window, a new desk and chair, and carpet. Your father will have half of a new truck by the time they finish with it at the body shop. I don't even want to think about what would've happened if you had been here. The timing of this trip was divine intervention in my opinion."

"How did this happen?" Jill asked.

"I spilled hot coffee in my lap, and I stomped what I thought was the brake," Dale spat out. "Can we move along to another topic now? How is Sally?"

"Well, Grandma and Anne threw a kegger last night while I was out. When I got back, Sally was stuffed full of old people, arthritis cream was flying all over the place, and someone stuck a cane through the bathroom wall."

Vivian found Jill's tale hilarious, Dale not so much. "Jillian, when I ask that question, I expect a full report. Have you been checking her oil and fluids regularly? Have you heard any grinding in the slide motors? Are you latching everything down before you take her on the road?"

Vivian scowled. "If I hear one more word out of you about your other woman, I will beat her eyes out when it gets back. I'm not joking, Dale. I will take a bat to that camper."

Anne nudged Ella. "Viv turns me on when she talks like that. I may be a lesbian."

"Oh, me too," Ella said and fanned herself.

"Did I hear Momma?" Dale asked.

Jill turned the camera on the phone and aimed it at the coffee-sipping pair. Ella waved and said, "Hi, son. Good morning, Viv."

"Are you making my daughter behave?" Viv asked with a laugh.

Anne shook her head. "That's a tall order. Shay had a makeover yesterday at a beauty shop with us, and Jill threw her in a creek, ruined everything."

"Is that the lesbian version of flirtation?" Viv asked.

Jill pressed the mute button and watched as her mother's mouth moved ninety miles an hour. She smiled occasionally, and her eyebrows wiggled every so often.

"Did you hang up on them?" Ella asked.

"I should've, but I silenced her instead. She's still going on." Jill watched the screen, then finally pressed the mute button again to turn it off.

"...I'm just saying you should turn a new leaf, baby. Carpe diem, carpe the woman."

"Thanks for the advice, Mom."

"Are y'all hitting the road today?" Dale asked.

"No, it's recuperation time for the terrible twosome," Jill answered with a smile.

"Are you purging the septic systems often?" Dale asked and dodged a swat from Viv.

Viv scowled and propped her chin in her hand. "We go from romance to shit."

"That's usually how it works," Anne added with a laugh.

"I empty the tanks regularly, Dad," Jill assured.

Viv shoved Dale out of the way, and her face filled the screen. "Where is Shay?"

"You should've asked that question before you went off a few minutes ago, Mom."

"Well, I figured you would've introduced us had she been around. Where is she? I want to see her."

"She's outside enjoying some alone time." Jill got up and went to the window.

Shay was seated at the table, the laptop open in front of her, totally unaware that Jill was watching her along with Viv, via the phone. Jill was about to tap on the window to get Shay to turn around when she realized what was on the computer screen. Shay was on the sex toy website and was apparently having a closer look at a purple and white swirled dildo because its small picture had been enlarged. Just as Jill grasped what she was seeing, Shay turned and noticed her. She slammed the laptop lid, and Jill turned from the window in a flash.

"That was her, Mom, and I need to get dressed now, so bye."

"All I saw was the back of her head and a flash of her face. Take me outside and introduce me to her," Vivian said excitedly.

"Now's not a good time, Shay's enjoying her...privacy, and like I said, I need to get dressed while no one is in the bathroom," Jill said with a nervous laugh. "Love you, bye."

Ella glanced up from the puzzle book. "That was kind of abrupt."

Shay didn't make eye contact with Jill the entire time they took the scooter from the back of the camper. Curiosity had gotten the better of her, and she wanted to know what Jill had bookmarked. And she got an eyeful—strap-ons, bullets, gels, and dildos of various shapes and sizes. It appeared that Jill was preparing to lay some kind of sexual siege. Shay knew that Jill had seen what she was looking at by the shocked expression on her face, and it was going to be awkward between them until they discussed it. So Shay decided to just put it out there.

"Nice day, huh?"

Jill nodded. "Yeah, lots of sun...kinda warm."

"I looked at your rubber dicks," Shay blurted out. "I know you know, and I told you I wouldn't, but the bookmark was just...right there. I had to click it."

Jill waved her arms wildly. "I'm not mad, if that's what you think. I felt bad for invading your privacy. I don't think my mom saw anything, she was too busy looking at you."

"Your what?" Shay practically screamed.

Jill blew out a heavy breath. "Oh, you didn't notice she was on Facetime."

Shay chewed her bottom lip as her blood ran cold, and she walked in a circle.

"This is funny. Let's just give the humor a moment to settle in." Jill folded her arms. "It's coming, just give it a moment."

"No...no." Shay shook her head vehemently. "It's not coming. I'm feeling white-hot shards of embarrassment and humiliation hitting me in the top of the head."

Jill grabbed a helmet. "Put this on. Embrace the hilarity."

"I think I could if my butt wasn't drawing my jeans up into my intestines."

Jill snorted, then bent over as she laughed.

Shay covered her face. "It's still not coming."

"It'll hit you later, I promise," Jill said as she tried to recover. She sniffed and wiped her eyes. "Nobody knows but us. My mother would've commented if she'd have noticed. She's as bad as Grandma and Anne and probably would've asked for the link."

A slow smile spread across Shay's face. "I may have a lot of questions for you later. You're stocking up on some serious shit."

"I enjoy sex, and I'm not ashamed to admit it, unless it's in front of Grandma and Anne. I don't want them thinking about what I do in the bedroom, and I sure as hell don't want to hear about their exploits. Trust me when I say they aren't shy about sharing their experiences." Jill picked up her own helmet. "You're on the back, I'm driving, and today, you'd better hold on to me."

It was a sunny day, and the rock wall-lined roads into town were scenic. Shay had on a pair of jeans and a T-shirt, but at times, she actually got chilly when they rode in the shade cast by the mountains. Her arms were wrapped tightly around Jill's waist, the warmth of her body helped ward off the chill.

"Movie first?" Jill asked when they'd stopped for a traffic light.

"Yes, unless you're hungry and would rather have lunch."

"The bacon and eggs are wearing off quick. Can you feel my stomach growling?"

Shay hadn't realized that she hadn't released her hold on Jill when they'd stopped. She liked the feel of Jill in her arms and the way they rode so snugly together on the scooter. At least, until Selene popped into Shay's mind, and she considered she was enjoying someone who was taken. She let go of Jill abruptly.

"Anywhere you want to eat is fine with me," Shay said, then wrapped her arms around Jill again when the light turned green.

Jill wheeled into a shopping center surrounded by restaurants and stopped near one of the buildings. "Do you really not care, or are you just being polite?"

"If there was something I was craving in particular, I'd let you know."

Jill pointed to a place across the parking lot. "There's a café over there with tables outside. Do you have any objections?"

"No, I think that would be great."

"Hold on tight," Jill said as she took off.

"What did you order again?" Jill eyed Shay's sandwich basket.

"Turkey on wheat with cranberry dressing. It's like Thanksgiving on bread. Do you want some?"

Jill's gaze was fixed on Shay's sandwich. "Yes, and I'll give you some of my club."

"Tell me about Selene."

Jill seemed surprised by the question as she accepted a piece of Shay's lunch. "She's...nice."

"I was just making conversation. We don't have to talk about her if it makes you uncomfortable," Shay threw out casually.

"It doesn't. We haven't been dating very long, and I'm...well, I'm still getting to know her." Jill pulled her phone out of her pocket, thumbed through a few screens, and handed it to Shay. "That's her."

Shay hoped her expression looked neutral. Selene's smile was perfect, makeup flawless. Her blond hair was perfectly coiffed. Even the lock that fell over her forehead looked as though it had been carefully placed to give her a casual but elegant look before the photo was taken. Just from looking at Selene's picture, Shay decided that she hated her.

"That was taken at her sister's wedding six months ago, but she still looks pretty much the same," Jill pointed out.

"You go for the ultra-femme, don't you?" Shay handed the phone back to Jill.

"That's what catches my eye first."

"How'd you meet her?"

103

"We have a mutual friend. He actually works in the same building as she does, so Cal is more of an acquaintance of hers. He found out that she'd broken it off with her girlfriend, and he told her about me. She was interested, so she gave him that picture, and he showed it to me. We all met for drinks, and I asked her out."

Shay took a bite of her sandwich and chewed for a moment. "So without ever seeing you, she gave him that picture."

"Yes," Jill said slowly. "What're you getting at?"

"I mean…she just threw it out there, like look at me, I'm hot. That says to me she's really fast or really desperate. Who keeps a picture of themselves like that readily available and gives it to strangers?"

"Nearly everybody on social media sites," Jill said with a smile that was a mixture of amusement and confusion. "When you get going, you really speak your mind."

Shay dropped her sandwich and pinched her brow. "No, that's a problem. Sometimes I say things the wrong way. I'm sorry."

"I don't think I'm seeing her anymore. I mean…I didn't call her last night. She hasn't called or texted me, either, so I think we're done."

"I thought you said you patched things up after Anne hung up on her."

"We did, she wasn't mad." Jill picked up the piece of sandwich that Shay had given her and took a bite, needing a moment to collect her thoughts. She chewed slowly, then said, "After our last conversation, I think we both realized that we were looking for different things."

"What was she looking for?"

"Sex."

Shay nodded with a smile. "Hence your shopping list."

Jill waved a finger. "Not all of that was for her."

"Stocking up for an orgy?"

"Oh, you're busting my chops today."

Shay lowered her sunglasses. "Are you into that, too?"

"You were looking pretty hard at that site too, so don't blow me shit."

"I think the fresh air has gotten to me."

Jill was laughing until she looked down at her phone and noticed that the picture of Selene was still on her screen. She pressed a button and deleted the image.

"I did not expect that to be a sad movie," Jill said when they walked out of the theater, and she put her sunglasses on.

"Sad? What part?" Shay asked.

"When the tree guy hit the ground and exploded into a million pieces and the raccoon was holding a stick and crying. It started off sad too, with that little boy and his dying mother. I do not like tearjerkers."

Shay laughed. "Oh, wow, you're a weenie."

"Hey! I heard you sniff when the raccoon was crying."

"Did you also hear the sneeze that came before that? This theater is way behind the times on its movies."

"Yeah, that's why admission is so cheap. We can see another one if you want. I'm using all the money I owe you on the bets," Jill said with a smile.

"Ah, so that's why you've been treating for everything. I want ice cream, the good stuff that comes from a parlor."

"We went down a street yesterday on the way out of here that looked like it had all sorts of cool stores, and I know I saw an ice cream shop. I think I know how to find it too. You drive, so I can look around and get my bearings."

When they arrived at the scooter, Jill handed Shay the keys. They put on their helmets, and Shay climbed on first. Jill got on next and wrapped her arms and legs around Shay like a squid.

"Jill, seriously?" Shay tried to put the keys in the ignition.

"You scare me."

"You suggested I drive."

Jill sniffed at Shay's hair that stuck out from beneath her helmet. "What kind of shampoo do you use? It smells great."

"Yours. I forgot to take mine into the bathroom when I showered. I can't drive with your foot under my chin, but I'll tell you what, you're limber."

"Oh, no, you're starting to sound like Anne," Jill said with a laugh.

"Then you'll really appreciate this. Get your monkey ass off me."

"That's not my ass pressed to your butt."

"Jill!" Shay laughed so hard she could barely start the scooter.

"I'm glad you came with us," Jill admitted as she wrapped her arms around Shay's waist. "Stay for the rest of the trip."

Shay glanced over her shoulder. "I'll think about it. Now which way do I go?"

"Take a right onto the highway, and I'll figure it out from there."

Jill wasn't sure what Shay's reaction was to her request to stay. She couldn't see her face, but she felt Shay's entire body stiffen, then relax when she made her plea. She liked Shay, plain and simple, and she doubted that it had anything to do with any ideas Ella had put in her head. They spent almost every waking hour together, and Jill didn't feel her usual need for space.

Once they were out on the road, Jill saw things that looked familiar and patted Shay on the shoulder. "Right at the next light." The buildings that lined the street were old and gave the area a quaint old-time feel. "This is it, let's park and walk."

Shay pulled into a parking space next to a Harley and killed the engine on the scooter. "Suddenly, I feel so small," she said as she waited for Jill to climb off the scooter.

They took off their helmets, and after Jill had stowed them, Shay casually brushed a lock of hair from her face as though she'd done it a million times before. She and Jill blinked for a moment in surprise. Shay turned and headed up the sidewalk. "I need ice cream."

"I know I saw a shop. We'll find it," Jill said as she caught up with her.

"Pizza, Chinese, Mexican, where's the fucking ice cream?"

Jill laughed. "I don't think I've ever heard you drop the F-bomb."

"I will use it liberally when faced with a situation that warrants it, and this certainly does. When a woman needs hot fudge, she fucking needs it."

Jill stopped in midstride when she noticed something in the window of a toy store. "Oh, childhood on a string! Do you know how long it's been since I've flown a kite?" she said before entering the store.

"I know I said I needed hot fudge, Jill," Shay said softly but followed Jill inside.

While Jill dug through a box of kites, Shay went to the checkout counter and handed her bank card to the clerk. "I'm paying for whatever the woman in the gray T-shirt brings up here, so please don't take her money."

"Oh, my God, a classic yo-yo!" Jill cried.

The woman behind the counter smiled at Shay. "Lucky for you, we're having a forty percent off sale this week."

One bat kite, yo-yo, and a pair of wax lips later, Jill and Shay left the store and headed to the ice cream shop. Jill clutched her bag happily and said, "Thanks for my treats. I would've only gotten the kite if I'd known you were paying for everything."

"You're welcome," Shay said with a smile.

They walked quickly to the ice cream shop. Jill got a banana split, and Shay got her sundae with plenty of hot fudge and two bottles of water. At the tables outside on the sidewalk, the pair began an intense pig fest.

"Do you still talk to your ex?" Jill asked out of the blue.

"No." Shay licked some of the fudge from her spoon and stuck it back into the dish. "Things got really bad right before I left. I was packing up my things the night before I left, and she got really hammered. That wasn't like her. The most I'd ever seen her drink at one time was two glasses of wine, but that evening, she killed an entire bottle. I think reality set in for her that evening. She got really belligerent, and I was doing my best to be considerate, but she said some hateful things. I lost my temper and said some mean things to her and she took it to a physical level."

"She hit you?" Jill asked coolly.

Shay released a heavy sigh. "This was not one of my shining moments. She swung and grazed my chin. Out of reflex, I shoved her and caused her to fall into a chair, and it broke. She completely lost her mind after that. She got up and was swinging her arms like a windmill. I couldn't get around her to leave the room, so I picked up a chair leg…and I smacked her in the forehead with it."

"No," Jill replied, drawing the word out.

"It wasn't that hard of a hit. Matter of fact, I wouldn't even classify it as one, it was more like a…bap. It didn't even leave a mark, but it stunned her enough for me to get out of there. I stayed at a friend's house, and the next day when I was ready to load the van, I had a small army with me. Chris pretty much avoided us, and she left without saying a word before we finished up."

"How long were you together?"

"A year and seven months." Shay opened her bottle of water and took a long drink.

"This is so good. If you want some, just dig in. I can't eat it all," Jill said. "I'm curious, do you ask women out, or are you more the passive type?"

Shay actually had to think about her answer. "I have, but I don't think I've ever just done it without some form of an invitation. If you're asking if I've just seen a woman I didn't know and popped the question on her out of the blue, then no. I'm not that brazen. Do you?"

Jill nodded. "When I was younger, I did. We used to go to a bar where they ID randomly. Some nights, I got in, and others, I didn't, but when I did get in there, I felt like I had to make good use of my time. Have you ever seen a woman you wanted to ask out so bad it drove you crazy?"

"Yeah," Shay said with a winsome sigh. "She belonged to someone else, though."

Jill waved her spoon with a grin. "Tell me the story."

"Why?" Shay asked with a laugh.

"I'm getting to know you, and I like hearing you talk. Regale me with your tale."

Shay propped her chin in her hand. "I have friends who were obsessed with softball. They played on a team called Spitfire, and the Vipers were their biggest rival. The woman who played first base for the Vipers was amazing, she had the longest reach.

I don't think I ever saw her miss a ball. She'd do impossible splits to make a play. She was tall and muscular, and at the same time, there was something really feminine about her. She was just a mixture of all things good. She had a confident air about her, but she never came across as arrogant." Shay's brow rose, and her eyes glazed over. "Her name was Ashley, and I had a mile-long list of things I wanted to do to her."

Jill pushed her ice cream away and opened a bottle of water. "So did you feel that kind of attraction to any of the women you dated?"

"Yes...well, maybe not that intensely. Ashley was a fantasy, and I knew I could never have her, so I felt free to mentally make her into what I wanted."

Jill nodded. "Makes sense. What do you want? What did fantasy Ashley have that the others didn't?"

"What all fantasy lovers have. She said and did all the right things. She listened to me, knew and loved me for who I was and not what she wanted to make me into," Shay said as a blush crept up her neck. She stirred her sundae but didn't eat any of it. "Tell me about yours."

"I can't because I've never had one."

Shay's eyes narrowed. "You're lying."

Jill was unable to hide her smile. "All right, did you ever see the movie *Rise of the Lycans*?"

"Yes, and I know exactly who you're talking about. That was one hot vampire."

Jill nodded. "I'd let her turn me into a vampire. Could you imagine eating an orange with those fangs? You could suck it dry and never have to peel it."

"Orange juice is your fantasy?" Shay asked dryly.

"My fantasy is the same as yours, except she stays with me forever," Jill said seriously. "Do you want to go back to the campground and break in that new rod and reel of yours?"

"Yes," Shay said with a smile as she stood and collected their trash.

"Can we use some of the fake eyelashes that Grandma got you for bait?"

"Sure, you may actually catch something this time."

Chapter 13

"You eat, then you fish," Anne said firmly. "I put my sauce on to cook right after y'all left, it's gonna be good."

Ella rinsed the pasta and smiled at Jill and Shay, who looked like a pair of monumentally disappointed children. "You have plenty of daylight left. You'll be out there right as the fish come in for their supper. Now go wash up for yours."

"I'll take the back, you take the front," Jill said to Shay. "We'll eat fast."

Shay stepped into the small bathroom off the kitchen and closed the door. She washed her hands, then splashed a little water on her face, trying to process all the events and conversations she'd had with Jill that day. When they'd first met, Jill was being a prick, and Shay was preoccupied with her dread of the trip, but a tide had rolled in so smoothly that the changes it brought with it swept Shay up before she realized what was happening to her. She was relaxed with Jill, intrigued with how her mind worked; she enjoyed every conversation and craved more. She'd been entranced.

Further contemplation was interrupted by a sharp rap on the door followed by, "Move it, tidbit, we have fish to catch."

Shay glanced at her reflection as she dried her face, wondering if Jill had intentionally set the proverbial hook that was in her lip. She didn't know if she should allow Jill to land her or fight it all the way.

"We're eating outside, take this to the table." Ella handed Jill a stack of plates with cutlery on top. "Come back in for another load once you set the table."

110

Jill frowned. "Can't we just eat standing up in here?"

Anne hit Jill upside the head with a roll of paper towels, then added it to the pile in her arms. "Get your ass outside and do what your grandmother said."

"Just for the record, I am no longer ten years old," Jill said over her shoulder as she followed orders.

"Take the glasses, please," Ella said when Shay stepped out of the bathroom.

Jill scowled as Shay set them on the table. "Wine? We're having wine too?"

"Shut up, you jackass," Anne spat out with her face pressed to a screened window.

Jill moved close to Shay. "I love getting her stirred up, that's how we express our affection."

"You could take the easy route and just...pick her a flower," Shay said with a smile.

"Eww, no. Anne and I don't roll like that. Watch this. Is there gonna be salad too? I hope you don't think we're gonna sit through coffee and dessert!"

"Jillian Savoy, you little shit, get your ass in here and carry out this food!"

Jill released a happy sigh. "She loves me."

"Well, I'm not going in there. You can hand me anything she gives you unless it's a ladle upside the head," Shay said with a laugh.

When the table was set, they gathered around it, and Anne made an announcement as Jill opened the wine. "I paid seven bucks for that merlot, so it's a good one. I hope you all enjoy it."

"It was less than that," Ella added. "There was a broken bottle in the case, and the labels on the others were stained, so the grocer let Anne have them at a steal."

Anne frowned at Ella. "But the original price was seven bucks a bottle, so that makes it the good stuff. Drink up, ladies, we have plenty."

"Cheers to that," Jill said with a grin as she filled their glasses. "All jokes aside, thank you for dinner. It smells wonderful."

Ella spread a paper towel over her lap and gazed at Shay. "So tell us what y'all did today."

"We had lunch, saw a movie, then ate more ice cream than we should have."

"Shay bought me a kite and some toys," Jill added. "I regressed to my childhood in a toy store."

"Well, I hope you're grown when you're shopping in the toy store online," Anne quipped with a grin.

Ella raised a finger. "I'm so fascinated by that harness and those bullet things. I imagine they're pleasurable for both participants."

"We're eating, drink your wine," Jill said with a scowl.

"No, I'm serious," Ella said as she put pasta on her plate. "The bullets vibrate, the dildo vibrates, that has to be one big shock of sensation even before you actually use the apparatus for what it's intended for. I assume you could simply put on the gear and have an orgasm without a partner."

Anne chuckled. "In the straight world, we call that premature—"

"Aaaaaaccccckkkk."

"Anne, we've been acked," Ella said with a laugh. "That was the noise we made when Jill got into things she shouldn't have as a child."

"When I was growing up, y'all taught me what was appropriate to discuss at the table, this conversation isn't. Now eat your dinner." Jill shot a look at Anne, who was shaking with silent laughter.

"I told you she would turn red as a beet, and look at her," Anne said and bumped Ella's fist.

Jill nodded. "Ah, all right, gang up on me, I can take it."

"I imagine sex is a lot less work with all that motorized equipment." Ella tried to keep a straight face as she said, "Do they sell bionic hips too? Because if that's the case, I'd like to place an order."

Shay cackled with laughter and covered her face with her napkin. Jill scowled at her for a moment before she caved and laughed. "Grandma, if I ever see them add hips to their catalog, I'll be sure to let you know."

Anne raised her fork. "I'd like a vagina transplant, so keep an eye out for that."

"Oh, me too." Ella covered her mouth with her hand and said, "I have no idea what we'd do with them."

"I'll tell you what, we'd get us some of them bullets and a warming dong. Ella, we'd burn them up on the first day," Anne squeaked out. "We'd have to demand a thirty thousand-mile lip-to-lip warranty."

Jill tilted her head toward the pair drunk with laughter. "I grew up with that."

"That explains a lot," Shay said with a smile.

Shay watched as Jill, backlit by the setting sun, moved farther down the bank in hopes of casting her line into a "hot spot." They'd been out there for almost an hour and a half without a single nibble, but unlike Jill, Shay wasn't disappointed. The weather was pleasant, and the lake's surface reflected all the hues of the sunset. It was a perfect ending to a great day.

Jill had turned and was moving closer with a look of determination on her face. She stopped and cast out her line, then held out her other hand toward the water. "The first fish that takes my bait gets an expense account and a new car," she said, sounding like a game show host. A few seconds later, her float went under. "Look, Shay, they're yuppy guppies!"

"You're adorable," Shay said much louder than she intended, but Jill didn't appear to notice as she reeled in her big catch.

"Sorry, I lied about the car and the money, but you do get a quick glimpse of life above water." Jill gently took the hook from the fish's mouth and held it up for a moment, so it could get a view of the land before she tossed it back into the lake.

"It was very kind of you to give it a quick tour," Shay said with a laugh.

"I figured it wanted to check things out. You know what we should do tonight?"

Whatever scheme Jill came up with, Shay knew she'd agree to it. "What?"

113

"Look at the stars already coming out, it's gonna be a beautiful night. Let's build a fire and roast some marshmallows."

Anne's head lolled forward as she drifted off to sleep. Ella gazed at her and said softly, "I can't believe she nodded off that fast. We took catnaps all day long."

"All the activity the last few days has caught up with her." Jill smiled as Shay handed her a skewer with a fresh marshmallow on it. "Thanks."

Ella watched the pair with interest. There seemed to be warmth and familiarity between them that wasn't there before. Jill and Shay sat so closely to each other that the arms of their chairs met. Jill roasted the marshmallows and fed Shay. Smiles and lingering looks were exchanged. Ella grinned with satisfaction as the seeds of romance she'd had a hand in planting started to sprout.

"Where are the UFOs we're supposed to be seeing?" Jill asked and stared up at the sky.

"There's some ledge the stargazers go to. Look at the brochures they gave us when we checked in, there's a map," Ella replied. "Bring your cameras when you go, you might catch something valuable."

A loud snore ripped through the solitude and startled everyone, including Anne. She sat up straight and scrubbed at her face. "Time for bed."

Ella stood and stretched. "Come on, you big ol' bear, I'm ready to settle in too."

"We'll do that," Shay said when Ella folded up her chair.

Ella patted her on the shoulder. "You're very sweet."

"That bionic hip would be especially useful right now," Anne said as she stood slowly with a groan. "You young'uns enjoy those healthy joints of yours while you can. Good night."

Arm in arm, Ella and Anne went inside the camper, and once the door was closed, Ella began to dance. "Did you see them?"

"The looks over dinner, little smiles, sitting so close they looked joined at the hip, hell yeah, I saw them." Anne joined Ella in her dance of triumph. "I told you Shay was perfect."

"You did not." Ella followed Anne to the bedroom. "I distinctly remember you saying this idea was harebrained."

"I don't recall anything of the sort. I must've been having a senior moment then. Switch off all the lights, let's see if they kiss."

"We're not gonna invade their privacy, we'll just grill Jill later." Ella grinned. "I like to see her squirm."

Anne laughed and dug her nightclothes from a drawer inside the closet. "We might get more information outta Shay. Those quiet ones are wild. You were that way when you were young."

Ella thought for a moment and remembered all the things she did in her youth. "You know, we might oughtta hook up Sally's water hose, just in case they need a cooling down."

"Are you having a good time?" Jill asked as she stoked the fire.

"I never dreamed I would say this, but I'm having a great time."

Jill sat back in her chair with a contented sigh. "I hope that means you'll stay because this is the best time I've ever had on one of these trips. This was not my idea of a vacation. I'd been making plans to go to Florida with friends later in the year. I felt obligated when Dad told me Grandma and Anne wanted to do this, though."

"You're making some great memories with them."

"I know, and I also know that's all I'll have to hang on to in the future." Jill inhaled sharply. "But I'm not gonna think on that now."

"What is Jill Savoy's crowning achievement?"

"Oh, that's a good one." Jill blew out a breath. "Let me mull that a second." A minute or two passed and Jill said, "I built a deck on the back of my house, and I know that doesn't sound like that much, but it was a big deal to me. I really didn't have any carpentry skills, and at the time, I couldn't afford to hire someone to do it. So I spent a lot of time watching videos until I was brave enough to buy the supplies. I built that deck by myself, and I felt like I had conquered Mount Everest. I know that sounds silly."

"You put faith in yourself, that's anything but silly."

Jill laughed. "Well, it's a real simple deck, no railing and just a few steps. Tell me yours."

"There are days I see this as failure and others as a testament to my character. I don't know if I can truly call it a crowning achievement, but it was definitely a defining moment. I've never even told Chloe this, and she knows just about everything about me." Shay subconsciously gripped the arm of her chair. "I worked in the recovery unit of a hospital, you know where patients go after surgery. I administered the wrong drug to a patient one time, and he almost died. On paper, I was sternly reprimanded and put on probation. The patient never knew what caused him to crash, nor did the family. My superiors and co-workers were very supportive, almost cavalier. 'Mistakes happen, you're human,' they all basically said."

"That's true."

"It is," Shay agreed with a nod. "I resigned, and my supervisor told me if every medical professional did that after a mistake, then there would be none left. This is why I sometimes feel like a failure. I know myself, though. I could never focus on what needed to be done without obsessing over making another mistake, and that would result in more. So I got into laser therapy and loved it because it makes people feel good about themselves."

"So being honest with yourself and doing something that elevates a person's self-image is your crowning achievement? That's pretty awesome."

Shay shook her head. "No, it's that I admitted all of that to you. I don't trust that easily."

"Well, I'm honored." Jill held Shay's gaze. "I think we need some of that expensive wine."

Ella sat up and grabbed her phone to look at the time. Anne sat up with her and said, "Do you hear that commotion, too?"

"This is my only complaint with campgrounds, there's always some asshole that ignores the quiet time rules," Ella snapped.

Anne got out of bed and pulled on her robe. "I'm gonna go out there and tune them up."

"Let's just call the ranger's station. You don't know what kind of people you're gonna be dealing—Anne! Well, wait for me." Ella got up quickly and grabbed her robe.

They walked out of their room and found empty beds. "Oh, shit," Anne said and marched over to the door. She and Ella stood there momentarily speechless.

"Bend over farther...arch your back a little...oh, that's good," Jill said just before she leapt over Shay. Both of them fell onto the ground laughing.

"Have both of you lost your minds?" Anne whispered loudly as she descended the steps and stomped out to the pair lying in the dirt. One of her bobby pins fell off, and the paper towel band wrapped around her hair dangled on the side of Anne's face.

Shay and Jill took one look at Anne and howled with laughter.

"You're drunk and too loud," Ella said firmly but softly. "Get up off that ground right now and go inside."

"Are we in trouble?" Shay asked, bleary-eyed.

"Yes, now get inside, or I'll hose you both down." Anne pointed at the camper. "I said git!"

Jill rolled and got up on her knees, her face close to Shay's. "Her Southern really comes out when she's pissed."

Shay raked a hand across her cheek. "You spit on my face," she said with a laugh.

Ella grabbed Jill by the shirt and tugged until she stood. Anne held out her hand and hauled Shay up. Both of them were covered in dirt, and Shay belched loud enough to shake the trees.

"I'm so sorry, that happens when I throw up," Shay said.

"Are you about to be sick?" Ella asked with concern.

"Oh...no, I already barfed." Shay tried to maintain her balance.

"Twice," Jill said and held up four fingers. "I don't think you have any more wine."

Ella took Jill by the arm and led her to the camper. Anne followed with Shay in tow. They herded the two into bed, clothing and shoes still on. Then Ella went outside to douse the fire.

Anne blessed them with a lecture. "I'll tell you what, you two are gonna be in some pain come morning, and don't expect any sympathy from me. I'll bet y'all disturbed everyone on this spur, and I won't be a bit surprised if we're told to pack up and leave."

"There are wine bottles all over the place out there," Ella said when she returned. "I think they drank every bit of it."

"I told you...outta wine," Jill said against her pillow, then giggled.

Shay raised her hand limply. "I like sporting goods stores."

Anne and Ella exchanged glances and shrugged. "Good night," Ella said and switched off the lights above their beds.

Chapter 14

Ella walked out of the bedroom the next morning and found what she pretty much expected. Jill and Shay were in the same positions as they were when they'd left them. Shay was spread eagle flat on her back, and Jill was on her stomach drooling onto her pillow.

Anne didn't bother to whisper when she said, "Shit on a shingle, would you look at the mess out there. We can't blame that on raccoons."

Ella sighed as she made coffee. "Well, we wanted them to have a good time, and they did."

"Hand me a trash bag, I'm gonna clean up the mess before everyone in the campground sees it," Anne said behind a yawn.

"No, wait."

Ella and Anne turned to find Shay standing behind them. Ella laughed and said, "My daddy used to have a saying, and it's very befitting right now. Your eyes look like two boiled eggs in a slop jar."

Shay grimaced and shivered as she put her hand over her mouth. It took her a few seconds to be able to say, "Don't wake Jill, I'll clean up everything."

"Oh, but we want to," Anne replied with a smile. "I composed a rousing serenade, and I was going to accompany it with a pot lid and wooden spoon."

Shay put a hand over her stomach. "Jill does all the driving, and she takes care of us and Sally, she deserves a break. Please let her sleep, I'll take care of the mess."

"That's very thoughtful of you." Ella handed Shay the bag. "I'll give you a hand."

"No," Shay said suddenly. "I may be sick again, you don't want to be around for that."

Anne opened the fridge and pulled out a bottle of water. "Drink this when you can, it'll help."

Shay pressed the bottle to her head and whispered, "Thanks," before she crept outside.

"I'll bet you they have sex before the end of this trip," Anne said softly as they watched Shay through the windows. "She's headed straight for the bushes, she's gonna blow."

"Oh, look, she's fallen right into that thicket. I hope there isn't poison ivy in there. We're gonna have to go get her out of there. I think she's still drunk."

"I think that headache powder that Ella gave me might be burning a hole in my brain," Shay said as she helped Jill string up her hammock.

"You were supposed to pour it in your mouth and swallow it with a glass of water, not snort it like cocaine."

"I know, but when you started gagging when you took yours, I couldn't help but laugh." Shay pinched the skin of her forehead. "I really think it's up behind my face somewhere."

"It made me giddy while we were changing the linens and cleaning up, but now I feel like a hollowed-out log." Jill sat on the hammock and tested it. "All right, there's a tender balance when sharing one of these things. We have to move as one."

Anne and Ella sat beneath the awning at the table. Anne held up her glass of tea and said, "I can't wait to see that."

Ella smiled. "Shay, honey, I really don't think you want to lay with Jill's feet in your face. She's got toes like a monkey, and I'm sure they smell."

"I don't have foot funk. Shay, just sit down and stretch out the same time as I do."

Shay mimicked Jill's every movement as they slowly positioned themselves, and once they were both settled, they

120

sported matching grins of triumph. Shay's smile faded when Jill said, "Now take off my flip-flops."

"I'm not touching those."

"Suit yourself, but I'm not gonna lay here with your dirty flippers in my face." Jill grabbed one of Shay's flip-flops and tossed it to the ground, then took off the other. "Talk about my monkey toes, you could hang from a branch with these."

"Don't touch my feet, Jill!"

"Are you tick—"

"Oh, did you see that roll, ladies and gentlemen?" Ella sounded like an announcer at a sporting event.

Anne joined in. "I'm gonna have to give that flip a seven. It lacked form. Neither of them had any control of their limbs, they looked like an octopus having a seizure."

"Now they're attempting a second try," Ella said. "I just don't see the potential for a gold medal here."

"Possibly a bronze," Anne added. "Oh, and they're down again. I think the team leader may've eaten some dirt on that spill."

"The American hammocker team is going in for another try. They're almost drunk with exhaustion, and I'm not seeing the same well-timed execution they exhibited in the first round," Ella continued in her announcer tone. "Shay is in—oh, it seems that the team members have turned on each other."

"Yes, but that toe pull was delivered flawlessly. Jill is dangling now, unable to right herself, and…she's out of there." Anne spoke into her glass as though it was a microphone. "That was a flawless dump on team Shay's part."

"That it was," Ella said with a nod. "Shay is dirty but undaunted as she goes for the goal again. Oh! Good block by Jill, and it looks as though she has scored a point of her own."

Anne gazed at Ella as she spoke into her glass. "I haven't seen this kind of action since team Shay executed a dive in the greenery."

"Jill is trying to use the toe pinch method to defend her position. I have to say, Shay is a force to be reckoned with. She's moving in with incredible speed. Jill is down! She is down!" Ella shouted. "Ladies and gentleman, what appeared to be a dull event has truly turned into an exhilarating struggle as Shay makes a dive for the goal, and she's in!"

"Team Jill is not out of the competition yet. Just look at the fierce determination. Shay is holding on like a spider—Jill is attempting the dump." Anne shook her head. "They're expending way too much energy with the laughter. Jill doesn't look strong at this point."

Ella shook her head. "I wouldn't count team Jill out just yet."

"That's right, Ella, the flip was flawless, and in one sweeping motion, team Jill is back on top. Shay is going for the Achilles heel...Jill's defense has weakened her position...she looks unstable...and...she's out of there."

"Team Shay is using pinecone missiles." Ella glanced at Anne. "Is that legal?"

"Absolutely. Team Jill is doing a fine job of dodging, and she scores again."

Anne and Ella howled with laughter when Shay stuffed one of the pinecones down the back of Jill's shorts. "Game over," Ella announced. "Team Shay takes the gold."

"I thought camping in an actual camper would mean we'd be less grimy. Why are we always so dirty?" Shay mumbled against Jill's calf.

"Cleanliness is for sissies," Jill said sleepily.

They had lain in the hammock curled around each other for over an hour dozing on and off. Both of them enjoyed the physical contact, even though it was marred by dirt and twigs. Shay's arms were wrapped around Jill's lower legs, and Jill's head rested near Shay's feet. Neither of them moved, afraid that they'd topple over again.

"You need to shave your legs. Quills are poking me in the cheek."

"Do you laser yourself?" Jill asked.

"Yeah, the last time I shaved was six months ago."

"Are you kidding me?"

"No, and stop moving," Shay said. "You're ruining my stubbly pillow."

"Does it embarrass you to have to...do someone's more intimate areas?"

"I was squeamish at the beginning, but now I'm so used to it that it doesn't faze me anymore. I've seen more naked people than Hugh Hefner. I will admit that it's not my favorite part of the job. I'd really rather work on tattoos. Just a word of advice, avoid the color green, it leaves a pale shadow unlike the other colors."

"I don't have any tats, and I don't plan to get any. I bet you take off a lot of names."

"All day long," Shay said with a smile.

"Does the laser hurt?"

"It depends on the person. I've had people jump off the table within the first few minutes of treatment, and others have told me it just stings a little. I did my legs myself, but another tech did my armpits, and that was kind of painful because the skin there is so tender."

"Have you..."

"Yep," Shay replied with a laugh. "I didn't do that myself, either. That's one place you really don't want to attempt alone."

"So you work with people who have been all up in your business?"

"Yes, we've all treated each other."

"Did you date any of them or any of the clients?"

"No, I never did. It's a real turnoff to heat up someone's butt crack with a laser."

Jill burst out laughing. "That is so gross. Please tell me you wear gloves."

"Definitely, sometimes two pairs, depending on the person. At the office where I worked before the move, there were two male techs, and they took care of the guys. But before that, I had to deal with male clients. Fortunately, most of them wanted back hair removed or tattoos that could be seen outside of their clothing."

"What kind of conversations do you have when you're doing this?"

"Some people don't want to talk, so they'll listen to music instead. Others will talk about movies or shows they watch,

123

what they do for a living, but mostly, they want to know all the things you just asked. I don't discuss the more personal procedures I've done. I don't do just hair or tattoo removal. either, though those are the most common. There's a laser that tightens facial skin, and for some people, it's almost like a facelift."

"You should see what I can do with a decimal point, it's stunning. Are you laughing? Shay, that's so not nice," Jill said with a smile.

Chapter 15

"Is it ready?" Shay asked as she stepped out of the camper with a platter full of burger patties.

Jill nodded. "Yeah, I'm ready to cook."

"I can do this. You sit down and relax." Shay placed the patties on the grill.

Jill held the spatula away from her. "I've got two jobs. I take care of Sally, and I do the grilling."

"I've eaten your steaks. I beg to differ on the latter part of your statement," Shay said with a laugh.

"You insulted my meat, you will not get this spatula."

Shay plucked the spray bottle from where it hung on the side of the grill. "You should use this more liberally. You let the fire get out of control, and it chars the food. Let me show you how," she said and shot Jill in the crotch.

"I'm gonna flip your burger, and I'm not talking about the one on the grill."

From inside the camper, Ella and Anne watched as Jill chased Shay around the campsite. Anne sighed and shook her head. "The damn burgers are gonna be like burned bricks."

"I think what we're seeing here is lesbian courtship," Ella said with a smile. "Jill is swatting Shay on the butt with the spatula while Shay is spraying her with a water bottle. It's sort of a mating dance."

"Ches used to bring me flowers he picked out of the neighbor's garden. I'm certain that took much less effort. Maybe we should sit them down and explain how things are done.

Otherwise, they may kill each other before they even go out on a first date."

"They've been dating since we left Baton Rouge, they just didn't know it at the time," Ella observed with a smile.

After dinner, Jill and Shay took a walk as the sun began to set. Shay had made the mistake of showering before dinner, and the sweet scent of her shampoo mingled with grilled burger. Jill inhaled deeply as she walked alongside her at a brisk pace. She hated the treadmill at the gym and avoided it as often as she could, but with Shay, Jill was content to walk for miles.

Shay stopped at a trailhead marked *Observation plateau, one-quarter mile.* "I think it's gonna be a beautiful sunset. Should we check it out?"

"Oh, yeah, definitely." Jill took the path without hesitation.

Shay followed. "It's gonna be dark on the way back. We should've brought a light, but I'll let you be first on the trail tonight. If you fall, I'll know not to follow."

Jill laughed. "I expect you to walk right over me."

"That's very chivalrous of you, but I meant ledges."

Jill stopped and Shay slammed into the back of her. "If we go, we go together, walk alongside me."

"Fine, but if you get us killed, I'm gonna be so mad."

Jill started walking again and asked, "What's been your favorite part of the trip so far?"

"When you freaked out about the snake."

"I was alarmed and rightfully so." Jill kicked at a rock on the path. "Pick something else."

"The square dance is another favorite. Oh, and your facial expression when Anne and Ella found your toy site."

Jill glanced at her. "I'm glad to know I gave you a few laughs."

"Many," Shay corrected with a smile. "You've made this trip truly enjoyable."

They continued on in silence as they strolled along the trail beaten down smooth by others who'd traveled it. The fading sun filtered through the trees and filled the forest with an ethereal glow. The noise from the campground, voices, and laughter faded as Shay and Jill moved deeper into the woods.

"Ha!" Jill patted a waist-high post with a light on it. "They anticipated goobers like us who come out here and get caught in the dark. I hope it's not crowded up there."

Shay silently agreed. She was looking forward to sitting quietly next to Jill and watching one of nature's most beautiful shows. Her hopes were dashed, though, when the trail ended at a plateau, and there were at least a half-dozen people gathered on benches staring out at the sky streaked with orange, yellow, and purple. Jill took her hand and went the opposite direction.

They climbed over a boulder and settled on a smaller one. "This is a good spot, don't you think?" Jill asked.

"Perfect," Shay agreed as they sat.

Jill sighed. "The sun is setting fast, we should come out earlier tomorrow."

"You're right, but look at that sky." Shay held her hand out. "Doesn't it seem like you can actually touch it from right here?"

"Mm-hmm. Do you ever wish you could travel into space?"

Shay shook her head. "No, I've seen the movies, it rarely bodes well for the traveler. Someone gets a hole in their suit, or they fly out of an airlock to drift into a cold dark void. I can see enough of it right here."

Jill laughed softly. "I think it's amusing the way aliens are depicted in movies. They're either drooling things with lots of legs and they eat us, or they're unisex gray-green bulbous-headed advanced beings. Granted, it's Hollywood's creation, but it's telling. Their heads are much larger to house the huge brain. The unisex body is supposed to convey that an ultra-intelligent species has dealt with discrimination and bias by eradicating difference. Wouldn't that be an incredibly boring world to live in? I like differences."

"Well, if they're anything like us, they'd find a way to one-up each other. They'd probably judge one another by the size of their heads."

"Right," Jill said with a nod.

"There are probably two bulbous heads sitting on a rock somewhere in the galaxy staring up into the heavens like we are

127

now, having this same conversation. They think we're more advanced because we have eyebrows."

Jill laughed and wrapped her arms around her knees. "Vacation is a good thing. You can take a moment to ponder the deeper meanings of the universe."

"Yeah, like the way airlines have us board planes." Shay continued to reach for the stars. "They should let the people with seats in the back get on first. The whole process would go much quicker."

"You're so deep."

"I know. I scare me sometimes. Aren't we supposed to be seeing UFOs?"

"Oh, I'm sure we will, right after Bigfoot does the hula on that boulder over there." Jill was quiet for a moment, then said, "You never asked what my favorite moment of this trip was."

"I was afraid you were going to say it was when you caught me looking at your sex toy site."

"That was a goodie, but I've given it a lot of thought. There have been many things, but my favorite was the night when we were Bigfoot hunting, and we leaned in to whisper to each other, and our lips touched."

Shay's hand slowly dropped, and she gazed at Jill. "Why?"

"Because it was hilarious," Jill said with a grin. "And it was the closest thing to a kiss…and I'd really like to do that right now."

Shay's lips slowly parted. "Why?"

Jill stared at her like she was crazy. "Because I like you. I'm attracted to you. Haven't you noticed?"

"I thought maybe—I hoped. Just do it—do it fast because I have the urge to run."

"Why?"

"Now you're asking questions? Just kiss me!"

Jill scooted closer. "Okay, I'm making my move. Oh, God, I'm nervous now. I may stiff lip you. Let me breathe for a moment."

"We're so getting an F in spontaneity." Shay shook her head slowly. "Maybe the reason we're so nervous is because this isn't right, it could mess up things. We're getting along so well, and now here's this moment of—"

Shay inhaled when Jill clasped her face in both hands. The kiss that followed made Shay feel like Jill had lit a fuse, and it quickly burned from her mouth to her toes. She jumped to her feet the second their lips parted.

Jill rose up on her knees. "What's wrong?"

"Great kiss," Shay replied as she waved her hands around wildly. "But we're on a trip that's gonna end, and now you...well, you already made me like you. That kiss, that's a whole new level." She threw her hands up, then darted into the woods behind the boulder.

"Shay, that's not the way we came in," Jill called out as she scrambled to her feet.

"Yes, I know that now," Shay said, already sounding far away.

"Let's talk about this. That's smart, don't you think?" Jill scrambled across the boulder and ran to the trail, hoping to intercept Shay. "Where are you?"

"Well, I'm not really sure."

Jill turned in a circle, unable to discern where Shay actually was. "Are you thinking that I'm just trying to get laid on vacation? If that's the case, I would've made a move much sooner than this. I like you, so please stop running around before you fall off something and die."

"I need time to process this. That damn kiss made me light-headed...and so did that branch...that's gonna leave a bruise."

Jill held up both hands. "Just stop."

"I'm not a Selene, you know. I love sex, I fucking love it, but I don't just do it randomly for fun."

"I just said it's not about that. Honestly, that's why I stopped calling her, that's not what I want. Are you cutting zigzags?"

"I don't know. It is *really* dark under this tree canopy. Keep talking so I can follow the sound of your voice."

Jill put both hands on her hips. "So, look...I think you should go out with me when we're out of the wild and if you survive. I think we have chemistry, don't you?"

129

"Yeah, but you know my history—that's a rock, okay, thank God. I've hurt people, and I don't want to do that to you. Besides, I think Anne and Ella would kill me, not to mention Chloe."

Jill moved farther down the trail as she listened to Shay stomping around in the forest. "Do you like me? Do you want to date me?"

"I found the trail light, I'm fucking blind now."

"Don't move, just stay right there," Jill said as she jogged down the trail. "I can't believe how fast you got down here."

Shay was standing with her back to the light and her eyes closed. "Is that you?"

"Yeah, are you trying to readjust to the dark?" Jill asked with a frown when she noticed a small scratch on Shay's cheek.

"I just need a minute, I'm still seeing spots behind my lids. I totally suck at making a dramatic exit."

"I beg to differ. The sound of you crashing through the forest was riveting. Why did you do it?"

Shay shook her head slowly and opened her eyes. "Because until that moment, this was a fantasy, and you made it real."

Jill stuffed her hands into the back pockets of her jeans to keep from touching Shay. "This doesn't have to be hard or complicated. We're friends, and if it doesn't work out, we'll still be friends." Jill shrugged. "Simple. Now let's get back to the campsite so I can check you for ticks."

"This is your romantic side?" Shay asked.

Jill kissed the scratch on Shay's cheek and took her hand. "It gets better."

"Is that them?" Ella pointed at the road.

"Looks like Jill's loping stride." Anne stared at the two figures as they drew closer. "I see Shay's yellow T-shirt, that's them."

Ella blew out a heavy breath. "Thank God."

"Do you two know that you scared the shit out of us?" Anne whispered loudly when Shay and Jill walked into the campsite. "Five more minutes, and we were going to call park management to form a search party."

Jill shrugged, unsure what the fuss was about. "We went for a walk."

"Three hours ago," Ella said hotly. "It's dark, we didn't know if y'all had been eaten by something or fell off a cliff. I called you a dozen times before I realized what that vibrating sound was coming from the table next to where you sleep. Then I called Chloe and got her all riled up because I needed Shay's number, and I found her phone stuffed in a shoe."

Jill bowed low. "I apologize. I'll be more responsible and considerate in the future."

"Me too," Shay added.

"Did you see any UFOs?" Anne asked.

"No, but Shay did an extensive search for Bigfoot in the woods," Jill answered with a smile.

"What did you find?" Anne asked seriously.

"Umm, a couple of rocks, a broken branch or two," Shay replied without cracking a smile.

Ella put a finger beneath Shay's chin and gazed at her face intently. "You've got a scratch. Why don't you give Chloe a call and let her know you're all right, then you shower first. There's no telling what you might've picked up out there. Jillian and I will stay out here and chat." She gave Anne the "you go, too" eye.

"Come on, kid." Anne threw an arm over Shay's shoulder as they walked to the door. "Tell me, did you find any scat?"

"I really don't know what Bigfoot shit looks like."

"I suspect it's bigger than other shit," Anne said as she climbed the steps with a groan.

Ella waited until the door closed behind them, then narrowed her eyes. "You didn't—"

"Are you really gonna ask me that?" Jill threw her hands on her hips. "All right, I have to admit you were right about my choice in women as of late, but when it comes to intimacy, I can assure you I know what I'm doing."

"All creatures can have sex. Anne and I watched a couple of squirrels do it today, it took about thirty seconds. I don't even think the female knew what hit her before the male ran off. I just

131

want to point out that Shay is not a squirrel, and you aren't, either, even though you act like one sometimes."

"Grandma, you understand that I do know the difference between the species."

"I just don't want you to mess this up by moving too fast."

"Thank you for your advice, and trust me when I say that I really like her, and I'm not gonna disrespect her."

Ella smiled and released a sigh. "I think she really likes you, too."

"I know she does, she told me right before I kissed her." Jill blew on her nails and buffed them on her shirt. "It was a good one too. I brought my A game."

"You get that from me. John used to say that my lips were as soft as a petal on a rose." Ella frowned. "Why do you look like you're in pain?"

"Are you about to get graphic?"

Ella folded her arms. "I don't think I like this double standard. You just boasted about your A game, but if I mention kissing my husband, you act as though I'd just passed gas."

"You're superhuman, I have you on a very high pedestal." Jill waved her hands around. "You can't be…carnal."

"I have news for you, honey, my sexual relationship with John is how your dad got here, and subsequently you, as well. So be thankful that I rocked your grandfather's world." Ella sauntered off and said over her shoulder, "I wrote the book on carnal."

Jill made a face. "I just threw up a little bit."

"What're you thinking about?" Jill asked.

Shay was lying in her bed staring at the ceiling with a slight smile on her face. "You know."

"Okay, but what part?"

"When I was stumbling through the forest, and I stubbed my toe on a rock at the same time a branch whipped me across the face."

Jill grinned. "I find your sarcastic wit so attractive. When you throw out those zingers, it's intoxicating. Your left eyebrow arches sometimes when you're talking, and I don't think you have any control over it, and I find that sexy too. At times, you squint when you're thinking about what you want to say, and that's absolutely adorable."

Shay rolled on her side and gazed at Jill. "I'm so flattered that you study me that closely."

"I notice everything you do." Jill inhaled deeply and let it out slowly. "I was so mad at Grandma when she brought you along because she and Anne are always trying to fix me up. I kept telling them you weren't my type, and to be honest, you weren't. You're not shallow or vain, you don't have to be dressed in designer clothes. You don't mind getting dirty, you enjoy simple things like fishing. You don't have to be reassured that you're beautiful every five minutes, even though you are. You're not anything like the women I've been dating, you're just perfect."

Shay's voice was hoarse. "I'll have to write down everything you just made me feel because I don't think I can say it without getting gooey weepy."

"I want to kiss you again." Jill hugged her pillow.

Shay smiled. "No, you have to stay over there because I might not let you go if you came over here."

"Grandma told me not to 'squirrel' you."

Shay's brow shot skyward. "What?"

"She and Anne saw two squirrels doing the deed, then the male squirrel ran off when it was over. I'm slightly offended she compared me to a hit-and-run rodent. I just want you to know that I want to share my branch and acorns with you, it's not just physical."

"That's…probably the most romantic thing I've ever heard," Shay said with a laugh. "I'd chew your fleas, groom your coat, and fluff your tail."

"Trust me, you've already fluffed it." The conversation was getting sillier by the second, and Jill couldn't contain her laughter. "I'd bring you sticks and leaves, and if I found a potato chip, I'd only hold it in my mouth for transport. You'd always get the first bite."

Shay snorted and covered her mouth with her hand. "I'd build you a nest with all you brought, and I'd shield you and the potato chip from the rain. I'd lovingly stuff my cheeks with nuts for you."

"Whatever you two are doing, knock it off. I can hear you laughing even with the damn door closed," Anne hollered.

"How about you meet me halfway for a quick kiss? You don't even have to get out of bed."

"You're determined to keep me up all night." Shay scooted to the edge of her bed, braced herself with one hand on the floor, and met Jill's lips. She lingered for a moment basking in the softness, then reluctantly pulled away. "Good night, Jill," she whispered as she settled back in beneath her covers.

Jill reached up and switched off the light above her bed. "I like you, I like you a lot," Jill sang softly.

"I can't think of anything that rhymes with lot except for spot and snot, but I like you too…a lot."

Chapter 16

"One more day here, then we'll head up to West Virginia," Ella said the next morning over breakfast. "Anne and I have made reservations at a beautiful campground on the side of a mountain, and there's a rocky stream that runs through the middle of it. The pictures are absolutely beautiful."

Beneath the table where they all sat, Jill's leg was pressed firmly against Shay's. The warmth and feel of her skin made Jill's pulse thud. She'd slept very little the night before while rehashing every detail of the kisses she'd shared with Shay. She'd drifted into the memory again when Anne snapped her fingers in front of her face.

"What?" Jill asked with a start.

"Do you need to go back to bed?" Ella asked. "I think you just nodded off."

"No, I'm fine. What're y'all gonna do today?"

"We met a couple last night while you two were playing in the bushes," Anne said. "Murphy and Sandra have a golf cart, and they invited us to take a riding tour of the park. I'll tell you what, the people who own this place have respect for those of us who can't walk very far. They've designated paths for carts, and we can hike on wheels. Ain't that fine?"

"I don't think I'm comfortable with you two riding off into the woods with someone we don't know," Jill said with a look of concern.

"We know 'em," Anne argued. "They're from New Mexico. He's a retired investment banker, and she was a violinist. They have two sons, five grandchildren, and one great-grandchild on the way. I'll tell you, anyone that can bake an apple pie like Sandra is good people. Jumping jalopies, that was good."

"He's got gout and can barely walk," Ella explained. "Sandra's no bigger than a minute. I'm certain that Anne could take both of them down if she had to, and if that's not enough, you know I always carry pepper spray in my purse."

"Can Sally haul a golf cart because I think I need one," Anne asked. "Is there such a thing as grand theft cart? How many years in the slammer would I face for that?"

"It would depend on whether or not you assault the owners when you stole it," Shay said.

Anne nodded. "I'll have to think on this because I do not look good in orange, and I really don't wanna rough up the old people. What're y'all gonna do today?"

Shay glanced at Jill. "I think we have a kite to fly."

The comment chased away Jill's grogginess, and she sat up straighter. "Excellent idea, and we could—"

Ella sighed as she picked up her phone and answered. "Hello, dear…what happened to your hair?"

"Viv decided she wanted to try something new," Dale ground out. "I ran away when she started to open a box of dye. How bad do I look?"

Jill leaned over and took a look at her father. "Do you remember what Sean Connery looked like in the movie *Red October*?"

Dale ran his hand over his spiky locks and said, "Yeah."

"Well…you kinda look like him, but your hair stalks are uneven. What'd she cut it with—the grass trimmer?"

Dale's frown deepened. "How's Sally?"

"Good grief, son," Ella said and rolled her eyes. "The damn camper is fine."

Dale ignored his mother and said, "Jill, are you hearing any grinding on the slides? You know we had that problem with the motor in the one in the bedroom a while back."

"It hums along just fine, Dad."

"How're my boys and the grandchildren?" Ella asked.

"Seth is walking mighty tall this morning. Aidan hit a grand slam at his ball game last night. I've had to watch the video half a dozen times this morning already. Will and Sharon are throwing a cookout tonight to celebrate the feat. Jude and Ricky packed up and went to Florida for a few days. I've been working on the renovations to your office, Jill. You can thank me now because your mother wanted to paint the walls what she calls mauve. I gently reminded her that you are a taupe woman, and I'm recovering from the pop knot of disagreement just fine."

Anne shoved her face in front of the phone. "Have you been checking on our house?"

"The alarm system and the forty-seven 'beware of dog' signs are doing their job," Dale said with a nod. "I've been putting your mail on the kitchen table. I took a look around inside just to make sure everything was okay, but I was afraid to touch anything because it's so sterile. Ricky's keeping the yard up, and he planted some flowers around the mailbox. It looks nice."

"Ricky is Jude's boyfriend," Ella explained to Shay. "We just love him."

"Tall, dark, and handsome is what he is," Anne added. "Jude knows how to pick a man."

"I'm still here in case y'all wanna talk to me, too," Dale said.

"Dad, did you check on my place?" Jill asked.

"I did, honey. You need to remember to take the trash out before a trip. It smells like a dead chicken in there. You got a package from DL Distribution, and I put it on your table."

"Oh, that's the toy—ow!"

"Jillian, did you just thump my mother on the ear?" Dale asked.

"She had a…a fly on it." Jill moved out of the way of the camera and ran a finger across her throat, then pointed at Anne and Ella.

"I know the weather is nice up there, but you ought not leave the door open. Don't y'all remember the time a raccoon got up in there with Viv? She nearly tore Sally apart."

"It was just one fly. It probably got in when we were coming and going. Sally is secure," Jill assured him.

"Where're y'all headed next?"

"West Virginia," Ella replied. "We'll stay there a day or two, then head back down."

"Y'all be careful, watch for snakes and bears and strange-looking people."

Anne laughed. "You just described everyone in this camper."

After Shay and Jill met Murphy and Sandra, they went off to find a place to fly Jill's kite. Jill was satisfied that the elderly couple posed no threat. She was, however, a tad concerned that Anne would convince them to allow her to drive their cart. She had been angling at that when Jill and Shay started out on their journey.

"Where are we gonna go?" Shay asked as she took Jill's hand.

"I was thinking about that meadow on the south side of the lake. I saw it when we were fishing."

"That won't be a bad hike." Shay gazed at the pack on Jill's back. "Is that heavy? Do you want me to carry it for a while?"

Jill smiled. "No, I got it. Hey, you know what else I've noticed? You don't have any more headaches."

"No, they stopped a few days ago. It's all your fault."

"I'm so not ashamed."

Shay contemplated all the changes that had occurred within her in the seven-day span. She wasn't tense or stressed anymore; a new tension had formed, and it was exciting. She wanted to tell Jill that she was experiencing all the things that Jill had admitted feeling when she met Jeri. This was where the dichotomy of their friendship became a little muddled. They'd discussed a lot of things, some very intimate and personal, but Shay didn't know how Jill would react if she confessed that she thought she was falling for her. Jill was the one with all the experience, and Shay trusted that she knew the difference between genuine feelings and infatuation. Those lines were still a little blurry for Shay. She stopped walking and wrapped her arms around Jill's neck. Shay kissed her slowly, pressing her body firmly against Jill's.

"I just wanted to see if doing that would cause all the sparks it did last night. It did."

Jill nodded, looking a little dazed. "Yes, it did."

"I'm not like you, I lack the ability to easily verbalize all the things I see in you. When I think about trying, it gets garbled in my mind, and I'm afraid that I'm going to blurt out something idiotic like 'you're so hot.' Does that make sense?"

Jill smiled. "I'm just happy to hear you think I'm hot, that's so much better than a dick."

Shay took a step back and released an explosive breath. "I did call you that, and I think you know you earned it those first couple of days."

"I was definitely in dick mode, but what am I now?"

Shay tucked her hands behind her back and scuffed at the ground with her shoe. "Incredibly sweet, charming, thoughtful, attentive, and you are so…you're really hot."

Jill laughed and grabbed Shay by the arm. "Let's go fly my kite. I can't stand here any longer without pouncing on you like a squirrel. I have to take Grandma's advice."

"Wow, the only life lessons I ever got from my mine were use cold cream daily and make sure you don't run out of cigarettes before nightfall because you're gonna want them with coffee the next morning. I only had one grandmother," Shay said as they walked into the clearing. "The other died when I was little."

"My maternal grandmother is a raging alcoholic. She and my mother don't have a relationship. I lucked out with Grandma and Anne, of course. They're brimming with wisdom, and they're eager to share whether you want it or not." Jill slipped the pack from her shoulder as they entered the clearing. "They just don't put into practice the things they teach for themselves. They can be rude and pushy, and they have no respect for anyone else's privacy. Would you like to hear a terrifying story?"

"My interest is piqued, but I can't deny that I'm a little afraid."

"My brother Seth and his wife have three kids. The youngest is six, and he loves going to Grandma's house. She and Anne spoil him, and he gets to swim all he wants. One morning, Amber, Seth's wife, was in a hurry to get the other kids to a baseball tournament, so she grabbed some clothes out of a laundry basket and threw them in a bag for Liam. What Amber didn't realize was she'd mistakenly included a pair of her underwear, a thong. Anne found it, and since she'd never worn one, decided to give it a whirl. After she'd tried on another woman's undergarment of a most personal nature, she returned it to Amber—she washed it first. But even the dryer couldn't shrink it back to what it was before." Jill laughed. "Anne isn't a big woman, but Amber is a size six. I'm sure Anne was sporting the mother of all muffin tops when she had on that thong. She said it cut off the blood flow to her head."

Shay rubbed her forehead. "I guess what stuns me the most is, not only did she try on someone else's underwear, but that she admitted it and gave them back. Are our underthings safe?"

"I think if she was gonna do a panty raid, she would've done it already." Jill held up the kite. "Good wind today, I don't think I'm gonna have to run to get this up."

All she had to do was let out the string, and the kite shot into the air. Jill fought a few currents before she made it to the end of the spool, then the black bat sailed high above them. She and Shay shielded their eyes from the sun and stared up at it.

"I remember this being much more exciting," Jill said.

"Hey, it's the simple things, right?"

"Yep," Jill said with a sigh. "Want to take the helm?"

Shay took the cardboard spool, tugged on it a few times to make the kite dip and dive, then she handed it back to Jill. "I'm done."

"I don't understand…this was awesome once."

Shay shrugged. "Maybe you had to put in more effort to get the kite up, and the feeling of satisfaction is what you remember. Think back to the last time you did it, where were you?"

"In a park down the street from our house. It was cloudy and windy," Jill said with a smile. "I was all by myself. I wasn't supposed to be out when the weather was bad, and a storm was definitely coming. I didn't have to run that day, either, that kite shot right out of my hands and went straight up."

"How old were you?"

"I had to be at least twelve because I wasn't allowed to go by myself until then. That was my first taste of independence. I couldn't go anywhere without Will and Seth, and they didn't want me around them."

"Was your hair long or short? Was it during the summer or winter?" Shay asked.

Jill looked away from the kite and smiled at Shay. "Why do you want to know?"

"Because I'm trying to envision you then."

"I was kind of pudgy, and Mom wouldn't let me cut my hair, so it was always in a ponytail, secured with those bands that had the plastic balls on them. It had to be summer because when it started raining, it felt really good. I was probably barefooted, and I wore gym shorts every chance I got and my brother's hand-me-down T-shirts."

Shay closed her eyes. "I have a great mental picture of that."

"You have to fly the kite now and paint a picture for me." Jill handed the spool to Shay again. "I'm already seeing long hair, a petite little body, maybe one of those matching short and shirt sets, all girly."

"Maybe when I was five or six. When I was around ten, I went to a friend's house, and we decided to cut each other's hair. She cut mine so short the stylist my mom took me to fix it had to use a trimmer on the sides. I thought it was the coolest thing in the world while I spent two weeks in my room, grounded. In public, my mom made me wear frilly things, so people would know I was a girl, otherwise I liked oversized T-shirts and those spandex-looking shorts."

Jill's gaze swept over Shay's gray cargo shorts and light blue T-shirt. Her hair was down and loose, resting on the top of her shoulders. "I...I have issues."

"What kind?" Shay made the kite go into a dive, then shoot back up again.

Jill filled her hands with Shay's hair and laid the first in a series of long steamy kisses on her mouth. The spool slipped from Shay's hand as she gripped Jill's waist. Even Ella's voice in Jill's head admonishing her not to be a squirrel couldn't help her rein in her restraint, but Anne's did the trick.

"Someone get a fire hose before these two burn down the forest!"

Jill abruptly pulled away from Shay and sounded confused when she said, "What the—why are you here?"

The elderly couple in the front seat of the cart stared open-mouthed. Ella and Anne sat in the backseat. Ella had a hand over her face, and Anne was cackling like a fool. Her laughter echoed through the woods.

"This is how old folks see the sights," Anne blurted out between gales. "Woo! You two certainly put on a show."

Jill waved weakly at Murphy and Sandra. "Um…good to see y'all again."

Ella pointed at something in the distance. "Your kite is in a tree. Why don't you squirrel your butt on up there and get it?"

Shay folded her arms and stared at the ground, and Jill dared to glance at the couple on the front of the golf cart who looked as though they were frozen. "Well…this is awkward," Jill said and rubbed her hands together. "Great weather we're having."

"Get out of the way, lovebirds. We're on a mission to see the flora and fauna," Anne said and jolted Murphy out of his stupor. The cart lurched forward, then sped off, but Anne could still be heard.

"Folks, on your left are pine trees. To your right is a pair of lesbians, and it's mating season. There's no need to fear them, they seldom bite or attack unless provoked."

Chapter 17

Anne watched Shay and Jill exchange looks over dinner that night. "You two are taxing the air conditioner. Your side of the table is ten degrees hotter. I felt it when I reached over there for the chips. Y'all just about killed old Murphy."

"Are you finished now?" Jill asked with a tight smile.

Ella threw in her two cents. "Some of my clothes are wrinkled, would you two mind standing near the closet and steaming them out?"

She and Anne bumped fists with matching grins.

Shay nudged Jill and said, "I've got one." She gazed at Anne as her left brow rose. "You may want to think twice about trying on our underwear."

"Touchdown!" Jill threw up her hands like a referee at a football game. "Spike the ball, baby, spike it."

"You're not supposed to be laughing at their zingers, Ella." Anne sneered and pointed at Shay. "You're fair game now, girl."

Jill flashed a proud smile. "She's proven she can handle it."

"Okay, on a serious note, we have to do some grocery shopping tomorrow." Ella tapped the list on the table beside her plate. We should keep in mind that we need enough food for a few days in West Virginia, and I figure on the way home we'll eat out more. Put what you want on the list, so we don't go into the store all willy-nilly and buy a bunch of junk."

"Where are we headed next?" Jill asked.

"Beckley, West Virginia," Anne said excitedly. "I found a coal mine tour there. Then Ella wants to go up to Canaan Valley. Y'all should take a look at the website we found in case there's something you want to see. That is, if you can keep your eyes off the dildo site."

Jill ignored Anne's jab. "We should get an early start in the morning. Everyone needs to be ready to roll by eight."

After Ella and Anne had gone to their room, Shay and Jill lay in their own beds facing each other. "We have to get up early, stop looking at me like that," Shay said softly.

"You're looking at me the same way."

"Yes, but I don't have to drive tomorrow. Close your eyes...make an ugly face." Shay laughed when Jill pulled her lips back into a sneer. "That's not even helping. What was in the box that arrived at your house, the one your dad put on the kitchen table?"

Jill's brow rose, but she didn't open her eyes. "Are you asking out of curiosity or fear?"

"A mixture of both."

"Nipple clamps, leash and collar, rubber duck, dominatrix suit, whips, paddles, hedge trimmer, dildos, thermal socks, a harness, chicken soup recipes...when're you gonna stop me?"

"I wasn't," Shay said sleepily. "I wanted to see how long you could go on."

"What's in your toy chest?"

Shay's eyes flew open wide, and she raised her head off the bed. "Oh, shit, my storage locker isn't temperature-controlled. I bet my rubber raccoon suit has already melted."

"I'm not gonna get a straight answer out of you, either, am I?"

"Not even a lesbian one."

"How did we go from insulting and calling each other names to this so fast?" Jill asked seriously.

"I marvel over that too. I actually felt a little pang of sadness when Ella mentioned going home in a few days."

"You said something last night like we're on a trip that will end. What did you mean by that?"

Shay ran her fingertips over the hem of her pillowcase and said, "I was speaking out of fear, afraid that what we have will begin and end on this trip. Jill, this is new to me. I go out on

144

dates, and I make a decision about whether or not I want to see her again, and it progresses from there. I never had time to decide that about you. I just know that I want to be wherever you are."

Jill smiled. "I feel the same way, and I had begun to think I never would again."

Shay exhaled loudly. "I need you to switch off that light above your bed and roll away from me because I want to come over there, and I know I can't."

"Yes, you—"

"I'm not in control right now."

"I'll just hold you, I promise."

"She's more sensible than you are, Jill. Tuck into your nest and shut up," Ella hollered.

"I hate Sally and her thin walls," Jill ground out and slapped at the light. "Quit laughing, Shay, and you too, Grandma."

Chapter 18

"You look like you did the morning you were hungover. Did you sleep at all?" Ella asked the next day as Jill readied Sally for the road.

"I'm fine."

Jill walked along, checking every exterior compartment to make sure they were secure. Shay did the same thing on the other side of the camper, and they met at the rear near the scooter. Ella had been keeping pace with Jill and turned on one heel.

"It's definitely lesbian mating season," she said when she found Anne in the kitchen stowing the dishes.

"Are they pawing all over each other out there in front of God and everybody?"

"No, but they look like they want to." Ella rolled her eyes. "I'm gonna have to coat them down in squirrel repellent."

"Lesbians move fast," Anne said with a shrug and continued packing up the dishes. "Jill taught us that U-Haul joke, remember. They go out on one date, and boom, they move in together and sort everything out later."

"I'm not sure that's the right way to go about things. I think they should really get to know each other before it gets physical."

"Ella, you can't go dropping old standards on people of today. Everything goes fast now. I can't even write a damn check at the store without someone having a conniption fit. Just think about this, Will met Chelsea in high school, then married her after college, and they divorced a year later. I don't think time has a lot to do with it. Sometimes we get it right, sometimes we don't."

"So what you're saying is, I need to leave the lovebirds alone and let them do as they please."

Anne nodded. "That's right, but you're not gonna."

"Anne, sit down until I get Sally stopped," Jill warned.

"I can't, I'm excited. They sell miner's hats here, you know the ones with the lights on the front. I'm buying everyone a hat."

"Don't waste your money on me," Ella said with a wave of her hand. "It'll just mess up my hair. We need to take a blanket. I read that the tours are very chilly inside the mountain."

Jill turned into a parking lot that wasn't very crowded and parked Sally in a place that would be easy to get out of. She looked around at all the old buildings with dread, knowing that Anne and Ella would want to explore each one. According to the GPS, Canaan Valley was only three hours away, giving them a lot of time to piddle around at the mine.

"Let's just remember that I like to have plenty of daylight to set up camp, and we still have to go grocery shopping. So—"

"They're already gone," Shay said with a laugh.

"I haven't even taken my seat belt off."

Shay stood and clasped Jill's face in her hands. "Good," she whispered before planting a toe-curling kiss on Jill's mouth. "Are you in a hurry to get into that mine?"

"No," Jill said numbly and fought with the latch on her seat belt.

Shay made no attempt to open the door and leaned against it with a smile. "You want another kiss?"

Heat rushed through Jill like a tidal wave as she pulled Shay into her arms. Their kisses were rough, and their hands roamed places they hadn't before. Jill inhaled sharply when Shay's fingers swept the skin of her sides beneath her shirt. Jumbled thoughts flooded her mind. Is this going to happen now, should I let it? she wondered before desire completely took her over.

Shay's teeth, lips, and tongue were on Jill's neck when her phone chimed indicating she had a text. She ignored it as she ran her hands over Shay's backside and pulled her snugly against

147

her. Shay was breathing heavy; she'd already begun to move against Jill's thigh when the phone rang. Shay groaned and pushed Jill away.

"Yes?" Jill snapped as she answered her phone.

"We got tickets for the next tour, it starts in five minutes. Hurry your ass up," Anne said and ended the call.

Jill clenched her teeth and her fists. "I swear they have some sort of sensor that lets them know when we're intimate. They've got—"

"I heard her. People in Montreal did too." Shay sighed and ran a hand through her hair. "I shouldn't have initiated that. I just couldn't help myself. You were so adorable on the ride up here, chewing the licorice like a rabbit. I like the way that shirt fits you, it shows off your—" Shay's eyes rolled up in her head when Jill grabbed her again and started kissing her neck.

Another text hit Jill's phone, and she laid her head on Shay's shoulder in defeat before having a look at it.

Bring a blanket...squirrel.

The car they loaded into for the tour had two long benches, and riders sat back to back. Jill and her group had a bench to themselves; behind them was a group of mostly adults except for a teen girl who didn't look very excited about the mine tour, either. Their guide, a retired miner, began his speech and spoke about the history of the mine, which was lost on Ella and Anne.

"I don't like your tone," Ella whispered with a frown. "It sounded dismissive, as though I'm not worthy of you."

Jill leaned close to them. "What're y'all arguing about?"

"Anne said we're a lot like lesbians because we live together and we share everything. Then she said she could never be attracted to me," Ella explained with a scowl. "But she said it rudely."

"Right, because she's straight, Grandma."

"But that's not how she said it. There was a tone."

"We're like sisters, I could never look at you that way," Anne whispered loudly. "Besides, I've never liked a ginger."

Ella gasped. "You always tell me my hair looks pretty after I've had it colored. Have you been lying to me this whole time?"

148

"I mean attraction-wise," Anne snapped. "When I was growing up, there was a redheaded boy who always threw rocks at me when I walked past his house. It left a mark in more ways than one. But on you, the red looks good. If it makes you feel any better, even at your age, you have a nice butt."

"I'd take that a lot better if you didn't say it with such condescension," Ella huffed.

"You didn't sleep well last night, you tossed and turned. You always get sensitive when you haven't had your rest, so stop taking your crankiness out on me."

"Anne Jacoby, you sounded like a man just then. And let me tell you, I could never be attracted to you, either, even if I didn't see you as a sister."

None of the women noticed that the car had stopped inside the mine until the tour guide cleared his throat loudly. Everyone on the bench behind them was looking over their shoulders at them. There were a few chuckles and snorts.

"Today, you'll get a glimpse of what it was like to work in a mine that was operational long before I ever took up the trade," the tour guide said.

As he continued, Ella and Anne picked up where they had left off more quietly. "So what's wrong with me?" Anne asked. "You got a problem with my hair?"

"No, your mouth, it's always open and full of shit."

"You'd be lucky to have a woman like me, Ella. As far as lesbians go, I think I'm a stud."

Ella laughed sardonically. "I hope they provide boots on this tour because the dookie is getting deep."

"Could you two have this debate later when we're not in a hole in the ground surrounded by strangers?" Jill rasped. "Behave, or I will separate you."

The pair quieted, and the tour continued. Jill and Shay were engrossed in what the guide had to say and didn't notice that Ella and Anne burrowed beneath the blanket until their snores began. Shay smiled at the tour guide apologetically. "At least they're quiet now…sort of."

149

"I have never been so embarrassed in my entire life." Ella held a hand to her forehead. She looked around the restaurant where they were having lunch. "I hope no one from the tour decided to come here."

"Who cares? We don't know these people, why should we be concerned with what they think?" Anne waved a hand at the basket close to Shay and Jill. "One of you monkey squirrels pass the bread."

"What exactly are you embarrassed about, Grandma—the lovers' quarrel or the snoring that threatened a cave-in?" Jill asked as Shay handed the basket to Anne.

Ella frowned. "You should've had the decency to wake us."

"I think the rest of the people on the tour were happy that we didn't," Jill said with a wink.

"I couldn't help myself." Anne tore a roll in half and smeared a little butter on it. "That mine was chilly and dark. I was warm and cozy beneath the blanket, and out I went."

Ella put her hands on the table. "Well, I just want to apologize for my behavior. Anne, you were right. I was tired, and that did make me cranky. Please forgive me for being an ass toward you."

"You're already forgiven," Anne said with a sweet smile. "I'll tell you what, you're the prettiest ginger I've ever seen, and if I was a lesbian, I'd probably have the hots for you."

"Well, that just warms my heart. You are a stud in a strong womanly kind of—"

"Oh, my God, stop." Jill frowned and waved a hand at the basket. "Eat your rolls."

"Don't interrupt when my woman is praising me," Anne said and jutted her chin. "Go on, Ella, honey bunny."

Ella jerked a thumb toward Jill. "Speaking of cranky."

"Are we staying at a state campground in Canaan?" Jill asked as she rubbed her temples.

"No, they're booked. Can you imagine the crowds? I found one that's privately owned," Ella replied. "From the pictures on the website and the way they describe it, it's a hideaway in the woods. This has been fun, thank y'all."

150

"We're not done, Ella, not by a long shot." Anne took Ella's hand and squeezed. "We're not out of the race yet. What's our motto?"

"No excuses." Ella nodded and brushed at the skin beneath her right eye. "No excuses," she said a little louder.

"What is this?" Jill asked curiously.

"We get a little down sometimes when we feel like the world is passing us by," Anne explained. "So we came up with the motto, and when one of us gets a little low, the other will remind her. There are no excuses not to get up and do something, no excuses not to learn something new. That's our little fountain of youth, and it's worked so far. We text, surf the Web, dance, and we travel. Ella's afraid this is our last trip, my job is to remind her it's not."

Shay fanned her eyes. "Oh, my God, I'm gonna get weepy."

"I'm going to the restroom," Jill said and promptly left the table.

"Give her a minute, baby," Anne said when Shay stood.

"I can't," Shay said and walked away.

Jill blew her nose and tried to force down the ball of emotion in her throat. Hidden in one of the stalls, she heard the bathroom door open and close, and listened as someone walked around. The sink ran for a minute or so, then switched off.

"Do you want to talk about it?" Shay asked.

"No," Jill said hoarsely. "I make jokes about them being old, but sometimes, I forget they're getting up there in age. They talk about watching me grow and how much I changed. I've been watching them change too. I don't know...this trip seems to have so much finality to it. Just like Grandma, I'm worried it might be the last."

"I understand." Shay leaned against the stall where Jill hid. "You've made it special. It's easy to see how happy they are and how much they're enjoying themselves."

Shay reached over the door, and a second or two later, Jill took her hand and held it tight. They stood there like that for a little while, neither of them saying anything. Jill breathed in, deeply drawing strength from the connection.

"Thank you for not making me talk about it," she said and released Shay's hand.

"Anytime."

Chapter 19

"That is not how you spell respect. There's no p z t."

"Ella, you sing it how you want to sing it, and I'll do it my way," Anne said defiantly.

Shay and Jill didn't hear the spelling debate, they were singing Aretha Franklin's *Respect* at the top of their lungs and dancing in their seats as Sally cruised blacktopped highways. When that song ended, Lou Christie's *Lightnin' Strikes* began. All four women came in on the falsetto chorus, but when The Cowsills' *The Rain, The Park & Other Things* played next, Anne and Ella knew every word and sang the verses with Shay and Jill doing a pitiful job on backup.

Ella fanned herself with a notebook and laughed. "Who knew that Sally could be a time machine too? Oh! Oh! Who can tell me who the lead singer of this band is?"

Shay pounded her hands on her lap. "I know her voice, I know who this is. Don't tell me."

"Here's a hint," Ella said. "The name of the band is the The Stone Poneys."

Jill shook her head. "That's no help at all, Grandma, at least not for me."

"It's killing me." Shay thrashed around in her seat. "I know this."

"Just not at this time," Jill chided and turned off the highway at the campground entrance.

"The website says we follow this road for a couple of miles," Ella said. "I think Shay is having some kind of fit."

Shay clutched her head. "It's on the edge of my brain."

"It rhymes with thermostat," Ella whispered.

"Linda Ronstadt!" Shay screamed, and Anne handed her a cookie.

"Oh, wow," Jill said as she slowly navigated the narrow strip of road. "There is nothing out here."

Grass and brush grew high alongside the road, and there were no signs. A few deer grazed near the tree line and seemed unconcerned with the camper slowly rolling past them. Jill was accustomed to seeing at least some evidence of mowing at the entrance of the campgrounds they visited. She glanced at Shay, who seemed equally disconcerted.

"They did say it was remote," Ella chirped nonchalantly. "Keep driving."

Jill drummed her fingers on the wheel. "If I end up in a place where I can't turn this thing around, I'm gonna be pissed. I'm not driving a Prius."

"I see something." Shay leaned forward. "It looks like the edge of a building poking out from behind those trees on the left. Do you need licorice?"

Jill held her hand out. "Yes, give me the grape, please."

"Don't fill up on that sugary stuff," Anne warned. "I'm cutting up carrots for the chicken potpie right now. Keep it steady, monkey."

"I'm doing my best." Jill pulled up next to a small wooden building that looked like an abandoned shack. "Grandma, did you get a confirmation on the reservation you made?"

"I did, and look, the sign on the window says 'open.'"

Ella grabbed her purse and was about to open the door when Jill said, "I'm going with you. Shay, if we don't come back out in five minutes, call 911 and send Anne in."

Anne moved up to the driver's seat where she and Shay watched them enter the building. "I don't know if that last comment meant that Jill wanted me to meet whatever fate they might face, or she thinks I can kick ass."

"It's the latter, I'm sure," Shay said as she stared at the door.

Anne adjusted the seat and looked as though she was about to drive away. "If they come running out, you grab ahold of

154

something because the second they get in the door, I'm gonna stomp the gas on this little lady."

Shay wasn't sure what scared her more—Anne in the driver's seat or whatever was in the shack. "She isn't little."

"I can handle Sally."

Shay rubbed her arms. "This is making my skin crawl. We just let them go in there," she said as she unclipped her belt. "Do we have anything we can use as a weapon?"

"The casserole dish could make a dent in someone's head. I'm thoroughly prepared to run down anyone who comes out of there besides Ella and Jill...well, Ella."

Shay was becoming more nervous by the second and looked at her phone. "I don't have much of a signal. I don't even know where we are. How would I be able to call for help?"

"Calm down now. We have to stay cool and collected." Anne shifted Sally into drive and kept her foot firmly on the brake.

Jill opened the door to the shack and held her thumb up with a smile. For half a second, Shay breathed a sigh of relief until Sally lurched forward, pinning her against the seat. "Anne, what're you doing?" she screamed, then nearly slammed into the dashboard when the camper came to an abrupt stop.

"I panicked," Anne croaked out shakily.

Jill ran over to the camper, yanked open the door, and stepped over diced celery and carrots spilled all over the floor. "What the hell is going on?"

"I was prepared to make a fast getaway." Anne started to vacate the seat without taking the camper out of gear.

Shay grabbed the dashboard. "We're rolling."

"Put Sally in park," Jill spat out, wide-eyed, then she was thrown forward when Anne did what she said without bothering to brake first. "Get. Out. Of. That. Seat."

"I'll tell you what, I've got this under control," Anne said as she gripped the wheel. "Where's Ella?"

"She's fine." Jill held out her hands as though she were approaching a frightened animal. "Anne, put her in park and stand up."

155

"I was driving before you were even a thought, Jillian Savoy, don't you bark at me."

Sally's side door opened, and Ella climbed in. "This isn't where we were parked before," she said lightly. "What happened to our vegetables?"

"Ask Anne," Jill said and climbed behind the wheel when Anne got up. She looked over at Shay, who had a curtain of hair covering her face. One lock in front of her mouth moved with every rapid breath. "You okay?"

"Linda Ronstadt."

The Wildlife Refuge for Humans was one of the most unique campgrounds that Jill had ever been to. Had it not been for Anne and Ella, she would've chosen one of the wilderness sites tucked in the woods away from the others. The grounds weren't manicured, there was no park or swings for kids to play on. There were only two bathhouses, and if Jill didn't have a park map to go by, she would've never noticed them camouflaged to look like the terrain. The refuge gave one the feeling of truly being in the wilderness until they approached the camping spurs, and she noticed the typical row of campers.

"You did good, Grandma. This place is pretty spectacular," Jill breathed out as she searched for the stone that contained their site number.

"Well, I wanted to avoid the typical, and this place sure seems to fit that description. That welcome center was certainly unique. The reception area was underground," Ella explained to Anne. "Jill took the spiral staircase, but I rode on a lift. The earth itself maintains the temperature, and I found it a tad chilly. The man that greeted us—his name is Charlie—said they use mountain water for the showers in the bathhouses, and it's warmed by the sun. They try to be as eco-friendly as they can."

"Found it," Jill said with a smile as she stopped and perused the site. They were on the end of a spur, and once Sally was in position, the side door would face the forest, allowing them some privacy. She backed Sally into the slip easily and released a sigh. "Time to set up."

"Well, hook up the water and electricity fast, we're gonna need to wash the celery you tromped all over," Anne said.

Shay got out of her seat and began to pick up the food. Anne followed Jill outside, and Ella prepped the kitchen for dinner. Once Shay had collected all the vegetables, she took the bowl to the sink and waited for Jill to give the signal that she was done hooking everything up.

"Thank you for sparing my old knees," Ella said as she watched Shay stare out the window at Jill. "She's precious, isn't she?"

Shay nodded and smiled.

"I think you are too."

Shay turned to Ella. "That's very sweet of you to say."

"I feel like I've known you for a long time now. Chloe has spoken of you often, and that's why I was looking forward to you and Jill meeting when she told me you were moving to Baton Rouge. I don't know if Chloe ever told you, but your weekly calls meant a lot to her. Your cousins do a fine job of seeing to her, but she considers you a friend, as well as her niece."

"I should've visited more often. The holidays were hard because I didn't have a whole lot of time off, and my parents wanted me to spend time with them. So my relationship with Chloe for years has been built over the phone. I know my being there kind of chases the boredom away, she's told me that, but I can't live with her forever. Do you think she understands that?"

"Sweetie, she knows you need your space." Ella patted Shay on the shoulder. "Just visit her when you can."

"Jill packed two bottles of that alcoholic lemonade and a blanket into that backpack she's wearing," Anne said as she and Ella watched the younger pair set out on their walk. "I don't think we're gonna see them for a while."

Ella smiled when she noticed Shay take Jill's hand. "They make a good pair."

Anne took a sip of her tea and smacked her lips. "They complement each other. Jill drags Shay out of her shell, and

157

Shay is pretty cool when Jill loses her mind. Shay's a lot like me."

Ella turned to Anne. "I'm more like Shay than you are."

"I'm cool under pressure, you have to admit that."

"No, I don't. Did you forget that just an hour or two ago you had Sally hopping all over the road for no good reason?"

"I was preparing to rescue your butt," Anne said indignantly. "You were taking off without me."

"My foot just got a little excited. I had it all under control. It's getting stoked up again, and I may plant it in your butt."

"I don't know if we should stray so far off the trail in the dark. You know what happened last time," Shay said as the light waned.

"I brought a flashlight, and we're coming up on the ridge that runs behind the campsites. If we have any doubts about how to get back, we'll follow it. I have an internal compass. I can find my way out of anything."

"Okay, good, because I didn't bring any breadcrumbs to leave a trail."

"How about here? We have an unobstructed view of the sky," Jill said as she stopped in the middle of a grassy field. "And we can still see where we came from."

Shay was fairly certain she was going to be seeing stars, but not the ones twinkling above. Nervous anticipation and arousal swept through her, and she no longer worried about getting lost. "Here is fine."

Jill opened the pack, spread out the blanket, and took out the drinks. "I stuffed a sweatshirt in the bag in case you get cold."

"You're very thoughtful." Shay sat on the blanket and watched as Jill opened the bottles. "I have to tell you that I have never spent this much time with someone and not craved alone time."

"Me either," Jill said as she settled next to Shay. "That's a big compliment to you. I get tense when I feel like I have to keep someone entertained. With you, I feel like…I don't know exactly how to say it."

"Sympatico."

"Yes, good word." Jill touched her bottle to Shay's and took a drink. Fluid spewed from her mouth half a second later. "Oh, wow, I have never drunk piss, but I'm sure that's what it tastes like."

"Is it that bad?" Shay asked and took a sip.

"You're even cute when you gag," Jill said with a laugh and patted her on the back.

"There's something wrong with this stuff." Shay wiped her mouth with the back of her hand and set the bottle aside.

"Okay, so much for enjoying a drink and stargazing." Jill propped her elbows on her knees. "We're just stuck with the stars and the bottle of water I stuffed in the pack."

"It's still romantic. Unless of course, a bear shows up. You didn't bring any food, did you?"

Jill pinched the skin of her forehead. "You said the B word, now that's all I can think about."

"Linda Ronstadt."

"Not helping."

Shay leaned over and kissed Jill's ear, then gave it a little nibble. "I think the only thing you need to be afraid of is me. Grrrrr."

"That was adorable."

"Wanna hear me growl again?"

Jill answered with a kiss, and Shay lay down, taking Jill with her. They were finally alone, free to explore the passion that had been building between them. Shay's hands were already inside Jill's shirt, blazing hot trails across her back and sides, her legs wrapped around Jill's. Her teeth, tongue, and lips teased the skin of Jill's neck, making Jill pant with excitement.

"I'm thinking about Grandma," Jill blurted out.

All grinding, kissing, and heavy breathing stopped in an instant. "Jill...that's gross."

"She's in my mind telling me not to do this," Jill admitted miserably.

Shay pulled Jill's head down onto her shoulder. "Talk to me."

"I keep hearing squirrel, loosey goosey, sugar addict, and I'm treating a filet mignon like a hamburger, all in her voice. It's

159

horrible. Then I think about what you said the other night about not being Selene, and I don't want to make you feel that way."

"If I felt that way, I wouldn't be lying here beneath you."

"Am I too heavy?"

"No." Shay tightened her hold on Jill. "Stay right where you are."

"I don't know what's wrong with me. I started feeling so guilty when I packed my bag of seduction tonight. I want you, but I don't want to make you feel cheap."

"You should've chosen a nice bottle of wine at the grocery store instead of that fermented lemonade."

"Stop it, I'm serious," Jill said with a laugh.

"I'm a grown woman, Jill. I knew what was going to happen when we came out here."

"This is a pivotal moment. Those are the ones you look back on and say, 'I wish I would've done that differently.'" Jill rose up and gazed at Shay. "It took me a long time to get over Jeri—years. I'm scared because I feel so much right now."

"Me too." Shay traced Jill's lips with her fingertips.

"I feel like if I connect with you on this level…it's just the last piece of me that I'm holding on to, and I want to give it to you, but I'm scared."

Shay nodded. "I understand that. It's ironic, isn't it? You're thinking, and I'm not. For the first time in my life, I'm just rolling strictly on feelings. I think we've done a role reversal."

"Tell me that's a good thing."

Shay pulled Jill down for a kiss. "It is."

"Are you frustrated with me?"

"Not at all. I can be content just lying here holding you all night."

Ella figured that Jill and Shay would get back late and reluctantly went to bed. She slept light and woke up often to check the time on her phone. At nearly three a.m., she got up, certain she would find the pair in their beds, and when she didn't, panic set in.

"Anne," she called from the doorway. "The girls aren't back yet."

160

"Jill says lesbians do it for hours," Anne grumbled.

"They left when it was getting dark, and in another few hours, it'll be daylight. Something's not right."

Anne slowly sat up. "Call her."

Jill had left her phone behind, much to Ella's disappointment, but she couldn't find Shay's anywhere, so she called it, and it went straight to voice mail. "Shay, this is Ella, call me immediately."

Jill was awakened by her own snore. She was flat on her back, Shay lay beside her the same way, their fingers entwined. Gently, Jill pulled her hand away to look at her watch and had to blink a few times to comprehend the digital number she was seeing. She gave Shay a gentle nudge.

"Shay, wake up."

"We fell asleep?" Shay sounded confused.

"We did, and hopefully, the worrisome twosome didn't notice. They'll have everybody and their uncle looking for us." Jill grabbed the pack and handed Shay the sweatshirt, then she emptied what was left of the putrid lemonade and stuffed the bottles into the bag.

After they'd packed everything up, they joined hands again. Shay started to go one way and Jill the other. "Where are you going?" Shay asked.

"Back the way we came."

"I think it was this way."

Shay yawned and scrubbed at her face. "You're probably right, I'm kind of groggy right now."

"This time, I had enough sense to bring a flashlight," Jill said as she switched it on. "All we have to do is find the path we made in the grass and follow it back to the trail."

"What about the ridge line? That would be a straight shot and quicker."

"I considered that as a last resort since we don't know what the terrain is like." Jill shined the light into the grass and found where it was matted down in places. "Here's our trail."

Hand in hand, they walked briskly through the field. The light illuminated what Jill felt was their path, but after a while,

161

she wasn't so sure what had made it. Shay picked up on it, too, and stopped.

"I'm very certain that we basically walked a straight line, this is curving right and left like it was made by a rabbit on crack."

"Okay," Jill said with a nod. "We did come from this direction, and we're still headed for the tree line. Once we get there, we'll walk along it until we find the path that leads back to the main trail."

"I'm good with that."

Jill squeezed Shay's hand and began moving again. "The high side is, the snakes are probably tucked away in whatever they nest in sleeping happily."

"They're most active at night, that's when they hunt."

Jill stopped again and released a nervous laugh. "That's some of that sarcasm I love, right?"

"No, I read it somewhere, but the weather is much cooler up here, and with it being early spring, they're probably not out yet. It's the bears that—"

"Don't."

"Sorry, I'm sure they're in a cottage somewhere eating porridge."

The light in Jill's hand flickered and went out. Neither of them said a word. Jill pounded it against her hand a few times, took a deep breath, and did it again. "This only happens in fucking horror movies with people too stupid to put fresh batteries in their lights. I took them out of the pack and shoved them in this bitch!" Jill yelled before she spiked the flashlight on the ground.

"I will find that battery rabbit on TV and choke the fur off of it," Shay ground out.

"The batteries weren't that kind."

"The rabbit dies, regardless," Shay said coolly. She took a deep calming breath and gazed up at the moon full and bright. "We have a nightlight above, and I have my phone, we can use the flashlight feature."

"What if we run that battery down and we need to make a call?"

"Moot point, I have absolutely no signal. We've got this. Let's just keep cool heads and find our way out of here."

They joined hands again and made their way to the tree line where they searched for the path they'd come in on. "You know what I like about state parks? There are signs everywhere." Jill studied the brush. "Speaking optimistically, though, when we do make love, it's gonna be awesome because we have some serious chemistry."

Shay pulled her to a stop. "You just shifted gears in one breath. Sex is on your mind right now, really?"

"I'm trying to take our minds off our dire situation."

"Jill, dire is a bear gnawing on one of us while the other runs screaming. We're kind of a little bit lost, don't use the word dire."

"You just used the B word," Jill said and stamped her foot. "Why does your mind keep going back to the B?"

"Yelling is going to draw the attention of the large and furry." Shay pulled her hand away from Jill and stretched her arms to the sky. "I'm taking a big deep breath, and when I exhale, I'll be calm."

"You say the B word again, and I will shit my pants, then I will not be calm."

"Another deep breath."

"Less breathing and more looking for the path."

"One more."

"Keep that up and you're gonna hyperventilate and pass out. Then I'm gonna have to carry you, and that will definitely be dire."

"Breathe with me."

"I am breathing! You can't hear it?"

Shay's arms were still up in the air. "I can't think when I get panicked, and you're making me that way." Shay gulped in a lungful of air and expelled it forcefully.

"Feel better?"

"I would if you would just—"

They both froze when they heard what sounded like something big moving in the brush. Shay could only imagine a bear heading straight for them and tried to recall a TV show she

163

had seen many years ago that told what one should do when encountering one of them. Nothing came to mind but a commercial with a dancing peanut. Slowly, she stepped in front of Jill.

"What're you doing?" Jill whispered so faintly, Shay barely heard it.

"Protecting you," Shay replied in the barest of whispers.

Jill promptly moved in front of her and put her arms out to keep Shay from moving ahead.

"I was a Girl Scout, I should be in front," Shay softly argued.

"Then you should've brought cookies to distract whatever that is out there."

A beam of light moved through the woods suddenly followed by a male voice that called out, "Jill? Shay?"

Jill's arms dropped at her sides, and she released a half sigh, half whimper. "Over here."

"It could be a talking bear with a flashlight."

Chapter 20

"Thank you, thank you, thank you," Ella said as she hugged Charlie, then Laurel, his wife. "I just can't express how grateful I am. I hope you'll turn a blind eye when I beat the crap out of these two women."

Laurel smiled, but Charlie had no sense of humor whatsoever and set his gaze upon Jill and Shay. "Next time you venture out, do it during the day, and take something with you like a strip of cloth to mark the trail. Be sure to collect them on your way back in."

"Yes, sir," Shay replied and hung her head.

"Have a nice day, ladies," Charlie said as he and Laurel climbed into their truck.

Ella waved until they were out of sight, then turned to Jill and Shay. "Inside, please."

"Now you're gonna meet the B word," Jill said lowly as she and Shay followed behind Ella at a distance.

"Does that still stand for bear?"

The door to the camper had no sooner closed when Ella began a tirade. "Y'all scared me half to death." She grabbed Jill's phone and held it in front of her face. "This is a *mobile* phone, Jillian, it's called that because you can take it most anywhere. If you two want to squirrel away, then Anne and I will vacate the camper, but you will not go back into those woods for a...for a—"

"Booty call," Anne supplied.

"There was no booty. We were watching the stars and fell asleep, then we got lost." Jill threw up her hands. "We didn't do

165

it on purpose. Just for the record, I'm about tired of hearing about squirrels. You know what, I'm a grown woman and—"

"We're sorry, it won't happen again." Shay bowed her head. "Really, really sorry."

Anne wagged a finger at Jill. "That's what you should've said. Next time your ass is in a crack, let Shay do the talking for the two of you because every time you open that yap, you dig yourself in deeper with us."

Ella stamped her foot. "We had to wake that man and his wife up to hunt for you. We've hardly slept all night because we were worried. Y'all should feel terribly ashamed."

Jill pointed at Shay, who said, "We do. I swear, we feel terrible."

"What do y'all want for breakfast?" Anne asked. "Ain't none of us gonna be able to get to sleep anytime soon."

"I am starv—" Jill clamped her mouth shut when she noticed the glare hadn't left Ella's eyes. "Was that a rhetorical question?" She pointed to Shay again.

"We'll cook," Shay said with plenty of contrition in her tone. "It's the very least we can do."

Jill did know how to scramble eggs and fry bacon, and she did that while Shay made biscuits and sliced fresh fruit. Breakfast was served at sunrise, and they sat outside beneath the awning to eat and watch it. Two minutes into the meal, Anne had strawberry jam on her napkin headband.

"I'll tell you what, you two gave us a good scare." Anne waved a piece of bacon and said, "I think this calls for special services. One of the lodges we passed on the way in here boasted a gift shop. I feel the need to do some looking around after a long nap."

"How're we gonna get there?" Jill asked and noted the scowl on Ella's face. "Okay, I'll button Sally up for a short drive."

"You don't have to do that, Charlie said he has a car he rents out to those that want to go into town, remember?" Ella said coolly.

Jill nodded. "I do now."

166

"But you will drive it and take us to anything we want to see," Anne added. "If we come upon a quilting class, you will sew."

"I am not—" Jill's nostrils flared as she exhaled and pointed to Shay.

"She will sew," Shay said with a nod.

"You will too," Ella added.

Shay clamped her lips together tightly, then said, "I will too."

Shay awoke with a crick in her neck just before noon. Jill had flopped down on her bed too tired to turn the covers down, and Shay just wanted to be close. She'd climbed in next to Jill and laid her head on her shoulder, and they'd slept for hours without moving. She sighed and remained in the cozy position despite the stiffness.

The bedroom door opened, and Anne walked out, dressed, Napoleon hair hat fluffed. Her stride slowed, and she held a finger to her lips when she noticed that Shay was awake. She walked over to the bed and kissed Jill softly on the nose.

Jill smiled and whispered, "Good morning."

"It's noon," Anne said, and Jill's eyes flew open.

"Did you kiss me?" Jill demanded as she sat up and dislodged Shay.

"I was gonna go for the mouth, but your breath is horrid. Do something about that, you nasty monkey, and while you're in there, wash your butt. We're going places today."

Jill looked around disoriented. "I was so deep," she said, then gazed at Shay. A slow smile spread across her face. "Hey."

Shay stifled a yawn and said, "Good afternoon."

"Do Ella and I have to leave the camper now?" Anne asked with a coy smile.

"I'm not feeling very contrite now that I've slept." Jill lay back down and wrapped herself around Shay.

Anne turned and walked away. "Oh, gross, it's monkey mating season in here. I'd rather watch Ella get dressed. I'll tell you what, her ass in granny panties is better than this."

"I'll tell you what, Jillian Savoy, you are cuddly."

167

Jill smiled. "You like it?"

"I do. I could get spoiled," Shay said as she snuggled into Jill's embrace.

"Good, then let me do it."

"Spoil me or cuddle me?"

"Both." Jill nuzzled Shay's cheek. "I'm sorry I got a little crazy on you last night when we were lost."

"I'm sorry for lying to you, I was never a Girl Scout. I did dress up as one—"

"That's so kinky."

"For Halloween, Jill."

Canaan Valley drew a lot of people in the winter, but in the summer, it was a sleepy little area, and most of the stores were closed in the off season. So they drove through the Allegheny Mountains stopping at every scenic overlook to gaze at waterfalls, deep ravines, and burgeoning foliage on the trees. Shopping was relegated to souvenir stores at the resorts.

"Love the bear, Jill," Shay said with a laugh as she aimed the camera on her phone at Jill, who was choking the stuffed animal. She moved in close to Jill and took another one of their smiling faces pressed together.

"Why do I keep hearing that James Brown song?"

"Because some idiot in the other aisle keeps pressing the button on a mechanical dancing bear," Shay whispered.

Laughter rang out followed by, "Ella, come see this, he's cutting a jig."

"I am not dancing with you in this store," Ella said. "Anne, no!"

Jill and Shay moved to the end of the next aisle and watched as Anne "shook a leg" to *I Feel Good*. Ella would try to walk away, and Anne would pull her back and give her a twirl. Ella finally caved and started swinging her hips with a grin on her face.

"I'm gonna film this and call it 'Old People Gone Insane' and post it on the Web," Jill said as she pulled her phone from her pocket.

"I need food, you know that I would now," Anne sang as she danced past them. "Somebody pick up my hip and follow me to the restaurant next door."

Ella fanned herself. "She is gonna sleep the whole way home."

"If I believed that were true, I'd buy that dancing bear to wear her ass out," Jill deadpanned.

Ella looped her arm around Shay's when they left the store and made their way to the restaurant. "Have you had a good time?"

"I have, it's been—" Shay looked over her shoulder. "Where's Jill?"

"She'll be along, I'm sure. I don't imagine she can get too lost between the store and the restaurant. I'm glad we have this rare moment alone," Ella said as they strolled along at a lazy pace. "I want to tell you something personal. Part of it you can't repeat, and you'll understand why in a moment."

Shay steeled herself for what she was about to hear and hoped that Ella wasn't about to admit that she also liked to try on other people's underwear.

"When I first met John, I knew in an instant that I was going to defy everything my mother taught me. He was tall and muscular, with a head of thick brown hair and the most dazzling blue eyes I'd ever seen. The slightest touch, a brush against my arm, or when he took my hand made me tingle. We had fire, and that's why I shunned my parents' wishes to marry another boy and eloped with John. The inferno blazed for a while, but when it cooled, I realized we didn't have very much in common. It took us years to develop a real relationship. Those were hard times," Ella admitted with a sigh.

"The story Anne told you about how we hit it off when we first met wasn't exactly true, at least not on my part. To be honest, and this is the part I hope you won't repeat, I didn't like Anne at all. She was loud and brash, pushy and demanding. I felt sorry for poor ol' Ches because he had to put up with her. I didn't even want to have them over for dinner that night, but I felt obligated because they had helped us move. One day, though, John and I had a fight, and I'd gone outside to cry my

169

eyes out. I was hanging laundry on the line just a-blubbering, and Anne showed up. She held me and listened to all I had to say, cried with me, told me all the things that Ches had done to hurt her. I realized then that her mouth was her first line of defense to protect her tender heart. We bonded then, and we were almost like lovers without the sex. We shared secret smiles, bared our feelings with implicit trust. She was there for me more than John could be, and I was the same with her."

Ella cleared her throat. "What I'm about to tell you may come as a surprise, but after I had Dale, if God told me I had to choose between John and Anne to spend the rest of my life with, I would've chosen Anne. That sounds like some sort of blasphemy coming from a woman who was married for most of her life. I loved my husband, still do, even though he's gone. He was a good father and an excellent provider who made it possible for me to live in comfort. He was loving in his own way, but we were never close friends. I'm not saying it's impossible for a man and woman to be friends, but when it came to us, we weren't."

Ella stopped walking and gazed at Shay. "I see the sparks between you and Jill, and I also see the bond of friendship growing. I hope the latter will continue to flourish because the former is going to fade. You have the potential to have the absolute best of both worlds, nurture that friendship."

Shay nodded slowly. "You just made me realize that I've been involved with a lot of Johns."

"Oh, don't say it like that, it makes you sound like a prostitute," Ella said with a laugh and resumed walking.

Shay opened the door to the lodge restaurant for Ella, who went straight to the hostess station and asked, "Did you seat a woman my age with large hair recently?"

It was obvious that the hostess was doing her best to suppress a laugh. "Yes, ma'am, I'll show you to the table."

Shay peered out the window by the door for any sign of Jill when Ella tugged on her arm. "She'll be along soon, sweetie."

After spending nearly every minute with Jill for the last week and a half, Shay actually missed her, and Shay wondered how she would feel once she got home. Jill would more than likely return to work, and Shay would renew her job search. She had every intention of dating Jill, but to Shay, that seemed sort of like going in reverse after basically cohabitating.

"Let's order, our sunrise breakfast has worn off, and I'm feeling puny." Anne handed Shay one of the menus. "Order for Jill."

Shay perused the offerings, unsure of what Jill would prefer. She'd decided that this was one of the pivotal moments Jill spoke of. Her selection would show if she'd been paying as much attention as Jill had. She glanced at Ella, who was gazing at her with interest, and Shay felt as though Ella was gauging her choice, as well. She knew that Jill liked beef, and the smothered sirloin tips would probably go over well, but they'd had burgers and steak recently. Shay began to get nervous as she debated between chicken parmigiana and the tips. Test anxiety had set in by the time the server approached the table.

Anne ordered first, then Ella, and it seemed the spotlight was on Shay. She glanced at the menu one more time and said, "I'll have the chicken parmigiana, and the woman who will be joining us will have the chicken fried steak."

"White gravy or brown," the server asked.

"White, and ranch dressing on her salad. I'll have the same on mine," Shay said as she handed him the menu.

"Did Jill mention that's one of her favorites?" Ella asked.

"I guessed," Shay admitted.

Ella nodded and smiled. "Excellent choice."

Jill arrived a second later with a big bag that she stuffed under the table as she sat down. "Did y'all order already?"

"Yeah, slowpoke, Shay got you chicken fried steak," Anne said. "They better bring out some rolls soon, or I'm gonna make a friend at one of the other tables."

Shay noted the pleased smile on Jill's face and mentally screamed, *score*. "What's in the bag?"

"Oh, it's a big—I'm not gonna tell you," Jill replied with a grin. "You'll just have to wait and see."

171

Chapter 21

"I'm not used to fishing in a stream," Shay said as she cast her line.

"Me either. We probably won't catch anything." Jill baited her hook and prepared to cast. "Hey, you wanna know what's in the bag?"

"Yes."

"It's a...you're not ready, and I'm not gonna tell you."

Shay knelt and splashed water on Jill. "You're such a tease."

"She's a jackass," Anne said. "You should've shoved her in."

Jill splashed Anne and Ella where they sat nearby. "This is my private torment of Shay, keep quiet or get wet."

"Ella, do you remember the time Jill demanded to be entered in a beauty contest?" Anne asked loudly, so Shay would be sure to hear.

Jill turned around and glared at her.

"Oh, yes," Ella said with a laugh. "She was jealous of a classmate who kept bringing her trophies to school."

"You what?" Shay asked with her brow raised.

"I was like six or seven." Jill held up a hand. "Don't judge me for my choices back then."

"The training was grueling." Ella smiled at Shay, who moved closer to hear the story. "Jill had a loping stride like her brothers, calluses on her hands from climbing trees, and her knees were always scuffed. She tasked us with transforming her into a prissy girl. Vivian was in absolute heaven."

"Misty Tyler called me ugly and stupid, and she had a freaking crown." Jill jutted her chin. "I needed to take her down a peg, so I submitted myself to the indignity."

"We had four weeks to turn a tough tomboy into a princess." Anne threw back her head and laughed. "We used the walk in front of the house as a runway, and Ella, Vivian, and I would coach her as she tried to strut her little stuff. She swung her arms like a monkey, hence the nickname. That child must have gone up and down that sidewalk a million times and never got it right."

"The day of the pageant, we painted her nails and did her hair, and she even sat still for the makeup, but you could plainly see it was killing her. And the dress, oh, the dress." Ella clutched her hands to her chest. "I thought the jig was up when we put that on her. Jill started to squirm and fidget like it was burning her skin."

"You were one beautiful little monkey," Anne said with a smile as she gazed at Jill. "Even still, we were nervous because you hadn't gotten the walk down. You tromped out to the car like a linebacker."

Ella nodded. "We all held our breath when they announced her. I was so afraid that it would scar her if she didn't do well. I didn't want her to think if she didn't win that she was ugly. Then, she strolled out on that stage with all the poise and grace of royalty, her head held high, a confident smile on her face. She took first place over Misty Tyler, who placed second."

"The pageant was on a weeknight, and they had to check me out of school to get ready for it." Jill rolled her eyes. "Mom was beside herself because she'd always wanted to dress me up, and she finally had her chance. She stepped into that classroom that day behind one of the ladies from the office and announced to everyone that I was gonna be in a beauty contest. The whole class laughed like it was a joke, but the next day when I walked in with my trophy, no one made a peep. Misty Tyler didn't, either, because she didn't want to admit that I'd beaten her."

"Wow, that was a lot of effort to take down a foe. I just blew up Jackie Schuller's dollhouse with a string of firecrackers."

Anne nudged Ella with her elbow. "She blows up shit, I forgot to mention that. Don't piss her off."

"I'm not surprised you won a beauty contest. I'm shocked that you entered one, but not that you won." Shay gazed at Jill next to a crackling fire that night. "What's in the bag?"

Jill laughed. "It's all about timing, Shay. You'll find out when it's right."

"I'm not going out with you when we get home if you don't tell me."

"Yes, you will."

Shay sighed. "Yes, I will."

Jill gave her a playful nudge. "Don't sound so excited."

"I don't know how I'll suffer through. We'll probably go somewhere with delicious food, you'll be charming and fun to be with. There'll be toe-curling kisses, and I'll have to muddle through somehow."

"I'm gonna feed you a bologna sandwich and make you do my laundry."

"Stop it, you're really turning me on," Shay said with a smile. "I'm getting excited about starting for home tomorrow."

"I'm not," Jill said seriously. "I've enjoyed having all your time."

"I was thinking along the same lines when we were at lunch." Shay scooted her chair closer to Jill's and laid her head on her shoulder. "I'm going to miss this."

"I have a big backyard, I'm sure we can set something on fire out there."

"You know I meant your presence…right, monkey?"

Jill chuckled as she stared at the fire. "You have got to quit spending so much time around Anne."

"I'm gonna miss her too."

"You think that now, but she's kind of like having syrup between your fingers after eating pancakes. The experience that put it there was enjoyable, but after a while, the stickiness becomes annoying."

"That's your best analogy?"

Jill thumped Shay on the leg. "You got a better one?"

"No, but I reserve the right to criticize yours."

"Hey, you two," Ella called softly from the doorway of the camper. "Don't stay up late, we have a long drive tomorrow."

Jill waved, and Ella closed the door. "Of course, she says that after we slept until noon today."

Jill followed Shay inside where they found Ella still puttering around in the kitchen. She smiled at them and said, "I was just doing some last-minute stuffing, so tomorrow morning will go quicker. I have truly enjoyed this trip, but I can honestly say I miss my bed. It's big and soft, and I don't have to share it with Anne."

"You shower first," Jill said to Shay. "I'll help Grandma get everything together."

Ella waited until Shay went into the bathroom, then motioned for Jill to sit. "Let's have a talk about friendship."

"Aw, shit."

Chapter 22

The next two days went by in a blur. Jill drove for nearly twelve hours the first one, which put them five hours out of Baton Rouge the next. The closer they got to home, the quieter they all became. Though Jill was eager to get back to her normal surroundings, she wasn't looking forward to having to say goodbye to Shay even for a little while.

Ella's friendship chat was somewhat of a revelation for Jill. Though the relationship with Jeri had truly been all about sex when they first got together, they did have a friendship at its base. They both neglected to nurture it as time went on. Jill realized she'd taken advantage of Jeri too often. She did things she knew that Jeri wasn't happy with but expected her to understand it was what she needed at the time. Like when Jill bought a four-wheeler when their finances were tight or joined a tournament softball team that kept her busy every evening and weekend for an entire summer. Jeri had been accommodating to a fault and eventually arrived at the crossroads of dissatisfaction and indifference.

She glanced over at Shay, who had her arms folded and her ball cap pulled down over her eyes. "Are you sleeping?"

Shay slid her hat up with her index finger. "Are you tired, do you need a break?"

Jill glanced into the mirror and noticed that Ella and Anne were asleep. "No, we're only about an hour out anyway. You know, I don't have your phone number."

Shay plucked Jill's phone from the console. She entered her number into Jill's contacts, then put Jill's in her own phone. "Now you have it, and I have yours."

"That was a pivotal moment. If you had changed your mind about me, you wouldn't have done that."

"What makes you think I put the correct number in?" Shay said with a smile.

"I'm having an insecurity moment."

"Good, that puts me at ease because I was having a tiny one too. Miniscule is a better word, no—infinitesimal."

"You may shut up now."

Shay laughed softly to keep from waking the pair in the back. "What's the first thing you're gonna do when you get home?"

"I'll start my laundry, then I'm gonna run to the grocery store and pick up a few things. After that, I'll probably have a bowl of cereal for dinner because I'm looking forward to something kind of light after all the rich food I've been eating. What will you do?"

"I'm going to try to find my bed and the rest of my clothes. I was in the process of trying to sort out what I needed for immediate use when I left on this trip." Shay sighed. "Tomorrow, I'll refresh my search for a job."

"Will you go out with me tomorrow night?"

"Yes, and any night after that." Shay rubbed her eyes. "This is making me emotional, I feel like I'm saying goodbye. I know we had lives before this, but I can't seem to really remember mine."

Jill reached her hand out. "Let's just agree to stay on this trip, even when we're home."

Jill parked Sally on the street in front of Chloe's house. Chloe came out to welcome them all back, and Ella and Anne tore out of the camper like two children eager to be free of confinement. Jill pulled the bag she'd been hiding out of a compartment.

"This is to remind you of when we got lost in the woods," Jill said as she produced a black bear and handed it to Shay. "I couldn't find the braided licorice sticks, but I did find a bag of green apple bites." Jill saved her favorite for last and pulled out a box. "You don't have to wear this, but I hope you'll put it somewhere you can see it often and be reminded of the fun we had."

Shay opened it carefully and smiled. "I had one of these when I was a kid with my name on it."

Jill took the simple leather band and snapped it around Shay's wrist. Instead of her name, it had images stamped into it. "The bear is again for the other night. The fish is for the times we went fishing. They didn't have an RV, so I got a tent, you get the gist, though. I put the little snake near the snap because I couldn't stand to look at it, and the smiley face is me."

"I didn't get you anything to commemorate the trip," Shay said with disappointment.

"You bought me a kite and a yo-yo and wax lips, which I look forward to chewing on in private. Not to mention a bunch of fudge at one of the places we stopped on the way home, but most importantly, you gave me two incredibly awesome weeks."

"You did the same for me," Shay said and wrapped her arms around Jill's neck as Anne, Ella, and Chloe gathered at the door of the camper.

"There she is kissing Jill," Ella said. "She missed you, and I'm sure she'll tell you that when she comes up for air."

"I see they've gotten very close," Chloe said with a laugh.

"They get any closer, we're gonna have to shut the damn door. Knock it off, you two," Anne barked out.

Shay reluctantly pulled away, hoisted the straps to her bag over her shoulder, and picked up her suitcase. "I'll see you tomorrow night."

"Yes, you will, and I'll call you this evening." Jill kissed her on the cheek and whispered, "Now I'm the one getting emotional, please go fast. Anne won't let me hear the end of it if I start sniveling."

"Walk around it a couple more times, Dad, there isn't a scratch on her," Jill said as she stood with her mother in her parents' driveway.

178

"When are you gonna clean her?" Dale asked.

Before Jill could retort, Vivian said, "You sent her on that trip, you clean the camper, Dale. Besides, nobody is going to get her clean enough for you."

"Mom, I can't visit, I need to get home, I'm tired," Jill said as Vivian took her by the arm and started leading her toward the house.

"I want to hear about your trip."

"It was fantastic, best one ever," Jill said as she veered toward her car.

"It had to have been, you don't look the same."

"Grandma told you, didn't she?" Jill said wryly.

"Oh, yeah, she was ecstatic. We all want to see you fall in love again and be happy, and from the way Ella described it, you're steadily rolling down that slope."

"I am, but this time, it feels so different. The first time it was like some wild magical thing. I felt like an adult for the first time. It was something I felt like I should do. You grow up, fall in love, make a life together. This with Shay makes me feel like a kid again. I flew a kite with her, simple experiences with her made me so happy, and now I feel like I left a part of myself at Chloe's."

Vivian smiled and hugged her. "Oh, honey, it sounds like you did."

Chapter 23

Chloe stood in the doorway of the laundry room and watched as Shay put her things in the washer. Her chubby arms were folded over her chest, and she was trying to look as imposing as she could at a mere five feet tall. She looked more like an elf in her red sleeveless shirt and matching shorts that hung almost to her knees.

"That was some kiss I witnessed in the camper, so you just go ahead and tell me all about Jill."

"Well, your plan worked. I met her, spent time with her, and now…" Shay held her hands up in front of her and watched them shake. "I feel like I'm going through withdrawal. It happened," she said in awe.

"What happened?" Chloe asked with concern as she moved close to Shay. "What's wrong?"

"I'm falling for her. What do I do?"

Chloe smiled at her like she was crazy. "You keep on doing what you've been doing, silly."

Jill ran a hand through her wet hair and put on her most favorite shorts that were at least twenty years old and had a big hole in the butt. They should've been retired long ago when they were a pair of sweatpants, but the worn fabric was as soft as it could be and perfect for lounging in when no one was around. The T-shirt she chose wasn't in much better shape.

As much as she enjoyed the trip, it felt great to be home. There was real water pressure in her shower, and her three-bedroom house felt like a mansion compared to the rectangular box she'd been living in. Jill actually petted her mattress when she changed her linens and told her bed how much she had missed it. Her sofa was given the same treatment.

"Oh, I missed you." She ran her hands over the tan fabric. "I'm gonna buy you flowers and set them here on the table so you can see them. Now let's cuddle and get reacquainted while I talk to my baby."

Jill flopped down and pulled her phone from her pocket. She'd waited until just before eight to call, so Shay could have time to eat, relax, and tell Chloe about her trip. She pressed the number, and it began to ring with an odd echo, and Jill wondered how she could hear the phone ringing in her ear and a muffled chirp at the same time.

"Hey." Shay sounded a little breathless when she answered. "I'm happy to hear from you."

"You sound like you're running around. What're you doing?"

"Well, something kind of crazy. Have you ever done something on impulse, and at first, you're certain it's the right thing, but then in the middle of it, you have doubts and you kind of panic?"

"Yeah," Jill answered with a smile. "What did you do?"

There was a moment of silence, then Shay said, "You have a really nice house, but your front walk is uneven, and I've tripped on it half of the forty-seven times I've paced back and forth."

Jill sat up. "Are you here?"

"Are you mad?"

"Of course not, I'm thrilled." Jill got up and ran to the front door, but when she opened it, Shay was nowhere in sight. "Where are you?"

"I kind of freaked out again, and I'm…well, I think I'm on the side of your house, it's kinda dark."

"Come back," Jill said with a laugh.

Shay appeared a second or two later walking fast with her phone still pressed to her ear. "We need to talk."

"Can we just do it in person now that you're here?"

181

Shay ended the call, stuffed the phone in her pocket, kicked her shoes off on Jill's porch, and walked right past her into the house. Jill stood momentarily stunned, then followed her inside.

"This is a nice house," Shay said as she spun in a slow circle taking everything in. "Your decorating style is kind of masculine with touches of femininity—don't touch me." Shay took two steps back and bumped into the sofa. "You're so good at expressing your feelings, you just put them out there. You're so brave. She paced around the room while Jill stood still and was completely flummoxed. "Is there a fish in here?" Shay asked as she stared into a tank.

"There was, but it died right before—"

"I've never been one to express myself very well, not like you. I was thinking about that tonight, and I realized that the reason I couldn't do it in past relationships is because I didn't feel all that much." Shay clutched the sides of her face pulling her cheeks down, making her features look bizarre. "But now I do. I've got feelings, and when I say what I think and feel, it sounds so stupid coming out of my mouth. I rehearsed. Am I a dork or what?"

She started moving again and picked up a photo of Jill's entire family from a table near a window. "I see a lot of your mom in you, but you really look like your dad. You know, it's like this," Shay said as she waved the framed picture around. "Everything I rehearsed sounds trite and hokey, like one of those teen romance movies that're so popular right now. Everything is *so* dramatic." Shay changed her voice and began to sound very much like Scarlett O'Hara. "I've never felt like this before. I do declare, I'm all atwitter. I can't eat, I can't focus on a single thing. We've only been apart a few hours, and I feel completely torn asunder."

"Maybe without the overdone Southern accent, it wouldn't sound so odd." Jill shrugged. "I'm just saying."

Shay continued her exploration of Jill's living room. "I really like that rug, the colors just pop out of it in contrast to the walls and furnishings. This is really scary shit. I don't feel in control of myself. I felt like I was having an out-of-body experience on the drive over here. It seemed one moment I was

182

in the car, and the next, I was at your front door, but I couldn't knock. I wanted to surprise you, then I worried that you'd think I was crazy or obsessive coming over here like this." Shay raised a finger. "But that's the problem, I am obsessing over—oh, this is cool, what is it?" She picked up an odd-shaped piece of glass. "Oh, God, I've developed ADHD."

"I found that in a burn pile when my dad was clearing the back half of the property behind the office. I have no idea what it was before it melted, but I liked the colors. Would you like something to drink?"

Shay thought for a moment. "My mouth is dry, but I don't know how to answer the question."

"I'm gonna get you some water to begin with and maybe something stronger to follow." Jill backed toward the kitchen. "You could sit down if you'd like."

"You know what's strange? There's not one thing I don't like about you, and usually, I have a whole list by now. What don't you like about me?"

"I haven't found anything," Jill admitted honestly as she took a glass from the cabinet and was blindsided. Shay had stalked her like a jungle cat and pounced. Enveloped in a flaming kiss, Jill's arms flailed for a second as she tried to set the glass on the counter. It toppled over and broke on the marble surface.

Shay broke the kiss, her lips already bruised, eyes wide. "I'm so sorry."

"Please say you're apologizing about the glass," Jill replied breathlessly.

"Yeah, so sorry," Shay said quickly before she kissed Jill and pushed away again. "Did you feel that?"

"How could I not?"

"Not the kiss, what's behind it?"

"Your body?" Jill asked dumbly.

"Jill, I'm not falling in love with you," Shay said shakily. "I'm pretty almost certain that I'm there."

Jill sagged against the counter. "You have got to learn to say things differently. When you began with 'I'm not falling in love with you,' my heart started to break."

"I told you that I wasn't good at expressing myself."

"No, you did great," Jill said with a smile. "I'm so glad you came over." Jill opened her arms, and Shay stepped into them.

Shay and Jill enjoyed what was really their first kiss. It wasn't hurried and breathless, but tender and sweet. It expressed what they both felt for a few precious moments before passion surged back in. Entwined in each other's arms, Jill led the slow dance toward the bedroom.

"I have to know one thing," Shay said when the backs of her legs met with the bed. "What's in the box on your kitchen table?"

"You'll find out later," Jill whispered against her neck as she kissed it, then pulled off her shirt and bra.

Shay's knees weakened when Jill's fingers grazed the bare skin of her chest down to her nipples. She sat on the bed, unable to stand, and watched in fascination as Jill stripped out of her own clothes. Shay reached for her, but Jill gently pushed her back onto the bed and pulled off her sweatpants.

Nothing had ever felt as exquisite to Jill as she lay atop Shay's bare body for the first time. Shay moaned into a kiss and filled her hands with Jill's hair. Jill marveled at the rush that swept through when their bodies molded together and their mouths joined.

Shay's racing mind quieted as Jill showered her in languid kisses, then began a slow descent down her body, gently stroking and kissing, whispering how lovely she was against her skin. She felt beautiful and cherished and believed every soft word spoken. She realized that Jill wasn't just trying to sexually satisfy her, but she was making love to her.

Jill's heart raced as she sucked one of Shay's nipples into her mouth, and she felt the rhythm of Shay's hips increase against her. She had no desire to tease, only to bring Shay to release and bask in that moment as long as she could as she slipped lower. The skin of Shay's abdomen was like velvet as Jill rubbed her face against her and tasted the sweetness of her skin.

Shay's eyes were open and unseeing as she ran her hands through Jill's hair. When Jill's tongue slipped through her wetness, Shay's mouth opened, and she made no sound, unable to believe how incredible the sensation felt. She clamped her eyes shut when Jill lavished the most sensitive part of her body with gentle strokes that slowly grew in intensity.

Jill released her hold on Shay's thigh and held tight when Shay entwined her fingers around hers. Shay's ragged breathing and the way her hips moved made Jill feel that she was right on the edge with her. She wasn't in control of Shay; Shay had complete command over her, and Jill did whatever her body dictated. Shay abruptly pulled her hands free and gripped the comforter on the bed. Jill's cry was louder as Shay shuddered against her mouth.

Chapter 24

"I'm sorry this is taking so long."

"No, I totally understand," Shay said with a smile to the receptionist. "I just took a chance coming in here. I really didn't expect an interview today."

"Dr. Lassiter wants to sit in, and she's almost finished with the patient she has now. I'll call you back as soon as she's ready."

"Thank you so much," Shay said and straightened her clothes for the hundredth time.

Shay drifted back into her thoughts that helped chase away some of the nervousness she felt. Every muscle in her body constricted as she mentally delved into the night before. The way Jill sounded, the smell and taste of her skin. The first time Jill came for her, Shay wanted to cry. The connection between them was so intense and perfect and exceeded everything Shay ever thought she'd felt with someone else.

"Ms. Macaluso?"

"Yes," Shay replied, still in the world of memories, and she jumped to her feet awkwardly.

"I'm Carla Pitre, the human resources manager, it's a pleasure to meet you." She shook Shay's hand. "Would you follow me, please?"

She caught a glimpse of her reflection in a mirror right before she stepped into the hallway that led to the offices in back. A deep red flush covered her chest and neck and was creeping up her face. She was about to step into an interview completely aroused.

"I can't find a damn thing," Jill said with her hands on her hips as she stared at the disaster area that buried her new desk. "But I have a window now."

"Way to see the bright side, baby." Vivian pumped her fist. "I'm going to leave you now to get everything sorted out."

"No, you're not, Mom. You've been working in here, and I need you to show me what you've done." Jill held up a form with doodles all over it. "This was important, it was supposed to be mailed to the Department of Labor."

"I did mail it, that's the copy."

"Here's a novel idea you should try in the future. After you mail a document, you file the copy, therefore it won't be just lying around available for you to draw on it what looks like deranged giraffes."

"That's a hyena," Vivian retorted. "I was drawing the mascot for Aidan's baseball team. Did you get any sleep last night? You're grumpy and dark under the eyes, which means you're tired or getting sick."

"Gwen," Jill bellowed.

"Yes?" Gwen said as she joined Vivian in the doorway of Jill's office.

"What are you working on right now?"

"My nails. One was torn, and it bothers me when I type."

Jill gazed at Gwen's clueless expression and sighed. "I need you to help Mom clear my desk while I see where we stand with the new accounting system."

Gwen shook her head. "I don't think you can, it crashed a few days ago."

Jill stared in horror at her mother. "Define crashed."

"Karen," Vivian called out loudly.

Karen's reply was muffled. "I'm not coming in there," she said from somewhere in the office.

Vivian threw up her hands. "Okay, it was my fault. We were uploading data from the old system, and there was an error. So I tried to run a report to see where the conflict was, but then the printer started shooting out paper like it was possessed. So I called Chip, the computer guy, and he had me do some things that didn't help at all, then your dad drove through the wall. So basically, we've been using the old system."

"Why didn't you tell me any of this before?" Jill asked as calmly as she could.

"Because you were on vacation. I did tell you about the window, though. It does add a lot of nice light in here, you have to admit that."

Jill clenched her fists. "Karen!"

Gwen looked into the hallway and said, "She just went out the side door. She started smoking while you were gone."

"Hey," Shay said with a smile later that day when Jill answered her phone. "I've been in an interview all afternoon, and I'm not even home yet. How about I just come pick you up and we'll go to dinner from your place?"

"I'm running late too. I was just about to call you. I say let's roll with your plan. How far away are you?"

"About five minutes, I think. How was your day?" Shay asked and slowed as traffic mounted ahead of her.

"I can't even begin to describe the shitstorm I walked into. My mom is pretty skilled at accounting. She and I used to work together before she decided she wanted to 'freelance,' as she calls it, which means she likes to sleep late, dabble, and not be responsible for anything. She is not a computer programmer and claimed our tech guy told her to change all sorts of settings."

"Oh, this story doesn't have a happy ending."

"The guy that sold us the software doesn't even know how to fix it. He had a team of techs in my office, and all of them were scratching their heads. I entertained myself by watching Dad walk around with his shirt zipped into his fly. The shirt was green, and the piece caught in his zipper stuck out about an inch. I don't know why I found it amusing, but I did."

Shay smiled. "I will drive tonight and you can enjoy some big girl drinks, then I'll let you go to sleep early."

"The latter doesn't sound all that appealing," Jill said as she stared at the shirts in her closet. "I'll admit now that I will probably try to change your mind about that."

"Three minutes out now."

Jill snatched a shirt off a hanger and shrugged into it as she asked, "I have two places in mind to take you for dinner, but I have to ask if you're craving anything in particular."

Shay grinned.

"I mean food."

"Are you watching me somehow?"

"I know you," Jill said with a laugh.

"Surprise me. I can see your house, so I'm gonna hang up now. I'll be there in a minute."

Shay ended the call, dropped her phone onto the seat, and pulled into Jill's driveway. By the time she got out of the car, Jill was standing on the porch. Jill's huge smile slowly slid off her face as she noted the outfit Shay was wearing. The blouse was a simple button-up, no cleavage showing, but the skirt hugged all of Shay's curves and revealed her nicely shaped calves enhanced by the high heels on her feet.

"This is…working Shay or wanna be working Shay?" Jill asked numbly.

"Wanna be. When I'm at work, I'm usually in scrubs." Shay hesitated when Jill continued to stare. "Is something wrong?"

Jill released a heavy sigh. "How hungry are you?"

"I can't believe I fed you hummus, chips, and cookies for dinner," Jill said listlessly as she lay with her head on Shay's stomach.

"Yeah, wasn't it great?" Shay smiled. "Who knew chickpeas were an aphrodisiac? We probably shouldn't have done this on your sofa, though."

"The cushion covers come off. I've washed them before when I spilled soup on one of them. Tell me about your job search today."

"I think I hit pay dirt. I emailed résumés to every job listing I could find, then I took a bunch more and hand delivered them to places where I'd like to work whether they had openings or not. Most of the time, they just took the résumé, but a few had me fill out an application, even though they weren't hiring right now. I was about to call it a day, and a woman called me from the very first office I went to. She was about to place an ad for an opening and wanted to know when I'd be available for an interview." Shay laughed. "Of course, I didn't want to appear desperate, so I went right back to her office."

Jill raised her head and gazed at Shay. "So you feel like it went well?"

Shay nodded with a big smile.

"I'm so proud of you." Jill kissed Shay's stomach. "I love the smell of your skin, and I want to take you to the bedroom and make love to you, but I can't hold my eyes open."

"I feel exactly the same way," Shay said listlessly.

Jill nuzzled the soft skin of her stomach and sighed. "Stay with me. I want to sleep cuddled up next to you again."

"I'd love to, but I'm gonna need you to carry me to bed, my legs are asleep." Shay raised a brow. "Are you laughing? Jill, this is where you say, 'I'd love to, sweetie, and even though you're light as a feather, I fear I would drop you and damage your flawless body.'"

Jill was half drunk with laughter. "Uh...yeah, what you said."

"Okay, well, feed me another cookie then. Don't put hummus on it this time, that was nasty." Shay threw an arm over her eyes and laughed after Jill stuffed a cookie right into the bowl of hummus. "You're eating that one, you jackass."

190

Chapter 25

"She hasn't spent a night here since y'all came back from vacation," Chloe said after she took a sip of coffee. "That's been nearly a month. Ladies, I think our girls are living together."

"We haven't seen Jill, either. Normally, she comes here once a week begging for food." Ella sighed. "I suppose Shay is cooking for her now."

Anne scowled and shook her head. "Well, this is just plain rude. Shay's basically using your house as a storage center, and we've had to freeze food because Jill wasn't here to eat it."

"Oh, no, I don't see it that way," Chloe said with a smile. "Her things are in storage, she just has some boxes and clothes in her room. I do miss spending time with her, though. The month that she was actually here was really nice, but I'm glad she's happy."

Anne waved a hand at Ella. "Get Jill on that video thing on your phone. I want to have a word with her."

"I'm not your secretary, Annabelle. You have a phone," Ella griped but did as Anne told her to anyway. She put on her glasses, and it took her nearly five minutes to figure out what she was doing, and instead of Jill, Vivian's face filled the screen.

"Hey, Mom."

"Hello, dear, sorry for the interruption, I was trying to get Jill."

"Jill? That name sounds vaguely familiar. Dale, do you remember someone named Jill?"

Dale's face appeared next to Vivian's. "Momma, you mean that urchin who used to hang around here?"

"I take it y'all haven't seen much of her, either," Ella said.

"We see her at the office," Dale replied.

"And neither of us has met Shay in person," Vivian added. "I've got a good mind to just go over to Jill's and demand to meet her. It's ten o'clock on a Saturday morning, surely they're awake by now."

"You promised."

"I did," Jill agreed and surrendered her free wrist.

She was completely naked, and Shay was tying her to the bed. She'd used two robe belts, a pair of stockings, and a tube sock. Jill pursed her lips and tested the bonds after Shay had finished.

"If you leave this room with me tied down like this, I will be pissed," Jill said, holding her gaze.

"You're very dominant in the bedroom, not that I have any complaints, but you don't give me very many turns to enjoy your body the way I want to." Shay's eyes sparkled as she said, "I've never done this. I never really wanted to until now."

Jill swallowed hard as she watched Shay open a dresser drawer. "When we talked about this, I had the idea that you would be the one in this position."

"You'll get your turn." Shay held up a purple and white dildo. "I still can't believe this is what was in the box."

"It warms and vibrates, and I was window-shopping on that website."

Shay crawled onto the bed between Jill's legs, vibrator in hand and a lustful gleam in her eye. Slowly, she lowered her head and teased one of Jill's nipples with her tongue before she sucked it into her mouth. She smiled when Jill moaned. "I love making you do that, and I'm about to make you do it a lot more."

Jill's eyes slipped closed when Shay kissed her mouth and nibbled her bottom lip. She could feel tremors in Shay's body as she lay fully on top of her. "Are you nervous?"

"Incredibly turned on," Shay answered against her neck as she kissed it. "Having you helpless like this has affected me more than I dreamed it would." She rose up and gazed at Jill.

192

"Are you having second thoughts because I don't want to do anything you don't want?"

"I trust that whatever you do, I will enjoy."

Shay smiled and rewarded Jill with another kiss. "Does it bother you to be helpless?"

Jill grinned. "I was helpless the day I met you."

"Oh, don't be sweet. You make me want to untie and cuddle you."

Jill's chest rose as she inhaled deeply. "Make me come."

"Please."

"Okay, you're taking this domination thing too seriously."

Shay laughed, then gave Jill a kiss that was a taste of things to come. Her descent down Jill's body was slow and deliberate. She teased Jill's breast with her teeth and tongue until Jill was breathing heavy and tugging at her bonds. Shay's heart was pounding in anticipation of driving Jill crazy. The muscles in Jill's thighs stood out as Shay slipped between them. She took a moment to trace them with her fingertips and enjoyed the way they twitched beneath her touch.

Jill clamped her eyes shut when she felt Shay's breath between her legs and shuddered when Shay's tongue followed and slipped inside her. As much as she didn't want to admit it, Jill was incredibly turned on knowing she was completely subject to Shay's whim. What thrilled her more was the idea of having Shay in the exact same position.

Shay had learned all of Jill's cues and pulled back when she knew Jill was on the edge. Every muscle in Jill's body stood out, and she trembled with each breath. It was a magnificent sight, and to be the cause of it was a high Shay didn't want to come down from too soon. She tested Jill's opening with the tip of the vibrating dildo, and Jill's moan shot through her, heightening her own arousal. She matched the rhythm of Jill's hips and slipped it deeper into her on each thrust.

Jill tugged at the bonds as Shay fucked her slowly, sometimes matching the pace with her tongue, but Shay would stop when Jill stilled for the impending orgasm. Jill heard herself begging, but the thought never crossed her mind, and when Shay

193

did make her come, she didn't recognize her own cries as they were wrenched from her.

Moments later, Shay appeared above her looking dazed, her chest, neck, and face flushed. "Untie me, and I'll make you come," Jill promised breathlessly.

A smile flickered across Shay's face. "I want to make you do that again."

"Untie me, please," Jill breathed out. "I said please."

Shay was clumsy as she fought with the knots. Her hands shook as she freed Jill's feet first, then her hands. Jill pinned her to the bed, kneeling between Shay's splayed legs, her head resting on Shay's shoulder, and she filled her with her fingers. Shay clamped her legs against Jill's hips and dug her fingers into her back. Jill was so out of control, she feared she'd hurt her. She slipped down, despite Shay's protests. She'd barely stroked Shay with her tongue twice before she came.

Breathless, they lay entwined when the doorbell rang nonstop. "That's Jude," Jill said after she caught her breath. "He has shitty timing, and he likes to ring that damn bell until it pisses me off. Maybe he'll take the hint when I don't answer."

The bell kept on ringing, though, and someone rapped on Jill's bedroom window. "Wake up, you bum!"

Jill stared at Shay in horror. "That's my mother, and she has a key."

"Shit," Shay whispered as they jumped up and scrambled to find their clothes.

Jill grabbed her robe, wrapped it around herself, and headed into the hall as she heard her front door open. "Mom, this really isn't a good time. Why didn't you...call?" Jill swallowed hard as she regarded the group standing in her foyer.

Anne gestured toward the floor. "Anybody ever tell you that you're supposed to wrap the belt around your waist instead of your ankle?"

Every ounce of blood that had been in the southern regions of Jill's body rushed to her face. "Um, hey...I'm just gonna go get dressed."

Vivian nodded as the others stared in silence. "Yeah, you'd better go do that."

194

Shay was in the bathroom dressed in a pair of shorts and a T-shirt washing her face furiously when Jill returned to her. "In the living room are my parents, your aunt, and Ella and Anne," Jill said and clenched her fists. "I went in there with my robe belt tied to my leg. Could you possibly dream up a more nightmarish scenario?"

"No," Shay said with a snort. "I'm just gonna stay in here."

"Oh, no, you're not," Jill said with a laugh. "We have to face this together. This is another pivotal moment."

When Jill was dressed and somewhat cleaned up, she and Shay faced the ugly music hand in hand as they walked into the kitchen where Vivian was making coffee and the others were seated around the table. Jill waved awkwardly. "Hi...family, so nice of you to drop in unexpectedly."

Vivian ignored her and gave Shay a hug. "It's so nice to finally meet you. Our rude daughter could've avoided this by bringing you to one of the many dinner invitations we've extended. Don't be embarrassed, at least Anne didn't catch y'all like she did Dale and I right in the middle of the act."

Anne closed her eyes and shuddered. "Oh, that was horrible. I would've gotten an eye transplant if I thought it would erase that image."

Dale got up and shook Shay's hand. "If you spend one hour with my mother and Anne, then meeting us is a cakewalk. It's a pleasure to finally meet you in person, Shay."

"Nice to meet you both," Shay replied, doing her best to maintain eye contact, then walked over to the table where she gave Chloe, Ella, and Anne hugs.

Vivian opened the pantry and proclaimed, "There's food in this house. Will wonders never cease? Who wants brunch?"

Chapter 26

Shay's pulse pounded in her ears as she tried to emotionally recover from dealing with her last client, who was extremely upset about the swelling her treatment had caused. She had less than a minute to mentally regroup as she pulled the next chart and gazed at it while she walked toward the reception area. She marveled at how just a name could chase away her tension and stress. She opened the door to the waiting room and kept her gaze on the chart as she called out, "Jillian Savoy?"

"Hi," Jill said as she walked over.

"Hello, Ms. Savoy," Shay replied as she would with any client. "How're you today?"

"I'm good, thank you."

Shay led her to one of the treatment rooms and closed the door after Jill stepped in. "What're you doing here?" Shay whispered and wrapped her arms around Jill.

"I want that patch of freckles on my chest removed."

"Seriously, they're going to charge you for this appointment. I have no pull here for special favors yet."

"I am serious," Jill said and pulled back to gaze at Shay. "Are you having a bad day?"

"My last client pitched a fit after her treatment because she had some swelling, and she had to go back to work like that. They explained that would happen when you told them what kind of treatment you wanted, didn't they?"

"Oh, yeah, before I saw you, they made me read stuff, then the woman who consulted with me went over the paperwork again. She reiterated that there would be swelling, and I'm not supposed to get in the sun after treatment. Some people bitch no matter what."

"I know, but I'm still new here, and I need to make a good impression."

"You've been here two months, baby, I'm sure by now everyone in this office knows that you know what you're doing. Now do me."

Shay laughed softly. "Do you really want those freckles removed? There's only four of them."

"They're big and ugly and can be seen when I wear a shirt with a collar." Jill touched Shay's face gently. "I want you to pretend that I'm some Jill you don't know and treat me like everyone else." She winked. "This is a fantasy, work with me."

"We cannot have sex in here," Shay said seriously.

"I understand, but we are when you get off work." Jill hopped up on the treatment table and held out her arms. "You don't know me, begin."

Shay rolled her eyes and looked at the chart. "Are you currently taking any medications?"

"I filled out the questionnaire, and I gave the same answers when the woman up front asked me all of this."

"Are you gonna play this as a dick?" Shay whispered with a laugh.

Jill shrugged. "I don't know, I'm getting into my character."

Shay went through her list of questions, and Jill answered each one. She made a few notations on the chart and said, "I'm going to step out of the room while you undress from the waist up. You'll need to remove all jewelry and any piercings you may have."

"You know I don't have my nipples pierced."

"Are you in character or not?" Shay asked as she laid a gown on the table next to Jill.

"I forgot! Okay, here I go...You don't have to leave for this," Jill said with a twinkle in her eye as she unbuttoned her shirt.

"See you in a few." Shay opened the door, smiled, and stepped out.

197

Jill completely ignored Shay and left her bra on, but when Shay stepped back into the room, she was wearing the gown. Shay washed her hands at the sink and asked, "Do you have any questions before we begin?"

"Do you have a girlfriend?"

Shay laughed softly as she dried her hands. "I do. She's extremely jealous and violent. She just got out of prison last week."

"I'd dump her ass."

Shay patted the table. "Lie back, please."

"I can't sit up for this?"

"You'll be more comfortable, and I'll have more space to work."

Jill opened the gown, and sticking out of her bra was a rose. "This is for you."

"You're so adorable," Shay said with a laugh. "But you have to take your bra off."

"Take the flower first."

Shay grinned as she tugged on the rose, and when it came loose, she realized a string was tied to it, and at the bottom dangled a key. "What is this?"

"Your house key." Jill took Shay's hand and kissed it. "I love you, Shay Macaluso. Will you officially move in with me?"

Shay blinked rapidly. "You're gonna make me cry at work."

Jill wrapped her arms around Shay. "Don't cry, you're about to shoot me in the chest with a laser. I need your vision to be perfect."

"I can't believe you did this here," Shay said into Jill's shoulder.

"Were you surprised?"

"Yes."

"That's why I did it."

Shay pulled back and quickly kissed Jill. "I love you too."

Jill buffed her nails on her shirt. "You found the right one."

"I did," Shay said with a happy sigh as she traced Jill's cheek with her fingertip. "Now take off your bra and lie down."

"Oh, you said we couldn't do that until we got home."

"I have to do your treatment."

"I love you, Shay, but do you really think I'm gonna let you light me up with a mini welding torch?"

Chapter 27

"In bed, really?" Jill asked excitedly and sat up.

Shay smiled as she set the breakfast tray carefully onto Jill's lap. "New Saturday tradition."

"Not that I'm complaining, but I was really enjoying the one we've been having."

Shay smiled. "Eat first, then we'll do that."

"Oh, that's a good idea. Eat, then exercise. You make me work so hard." Jill threw an arm across her forehead. "Hours of lovemaking are so strenuous."

Shay pointed to a pill on Jill's plate. "That's why you're going to take that vitamin."

"You've been spending way too much time with Grandma and Anne."

Shay picked up a forkful of eggs and fed it to Jill. "I want to keep you healthy, so I can wear you down at night and in the mornings."

Jill chewed slowly and swallowed. "You make me happy."

"Even when we're doing laundry?"

"Yep."

"When we're washing dishes?"

"Yep."

"When we clean the bathrooms?"

"Okay, maybe not then. I will admit, though, household chores are much more fun with you around. They'd be even better if you'd agree to do them in the buff."

"There's good naked and there's bad, me bent over scrubbing the tub would fall into the bad category."

"That's your opinion," Jill said with a laugh as she fed Shay a strawberry. "No chores today, though, we have a pool party to attend. You're gonna meet the whole Savoy brood, and I hope you'll still love me afterward."

"Nothing's gonna change that."

"I'll need that reassurance when we get home tonight. When will I meet your family?"

Shay frowned. "Probably sometime during the holidays, and I'll need your reassurance then. My mom is shy and quiet, so Dad does all the talking, and I've already told you about my brother and sister. There's a good chance they won't go to Mom and Dad's if they know I'm bringing you. It's nothing to do with you personally, that's just the way they are. I'm so sorry."

Jill nodded and brushed Shay's cheek with the backs of her fingers. "I know people like that. Don't apologize for them. That's their choice, but in my opinion, they're missing out because we're pretty spectacular."

Shay smiled as she took Jill's hand and kissed it. "I think you are. Sometimes I have a hard time believing that just a few months ago I'd pretty much given up on relationships and love, now I'm in the middle of both."

"You sure took me by surprise. Between me and you, Grandma and Chloe made a perfect match."

Shay leaned over and kissed Jill. The tray on Jill's lap shifted and slid off the side of the bed sending eggs, coffee, and fruit flying all over the floor. Neither of them noticed.

After meeting Will and Seth, Shay completely understood why Jill and Jude called them pricks. They were loud and brutish, but their wives Amber and Sharon were polite and very welcoming. There were kids everywhere, and Shay figured by the end of the day she'd commit all of their names to memory. Her favorite of the Savoy children, aside from Jill, was Jude. When they were introduced, Jude had wrapped her in a big hug and whispered, "Thank you for making my sister so happy, I love you already." Shay joyfully realized that she'd gained two new brothers, Jude and his partner, Ricky.

After the introductions and everyone had gone outside to the pool, Anne took Shay by the hand and said, "I want to show you something." Shay followed Anne into her bedroom and marveled at all the framed photos on her wall.

"Some people decorate with paintings or flowers, but I do it with life. This has been mine."

"Wow," Shay said in awe and stared at the wall of mostly black and white photos. She saw Anne as a child, then a young woman with a nice-looking man at her side the day they were married. There were plenty of photos with Ella and John, too. "Ches was handsome."

"Yes, he was," Anne agreed with a somber smile.

There were so many pictures of Anne and Ella together that Shay couldn't count them all. Both of the women aged as Shay slowly moved to the next wall where she saw photos of Dale and Vivian's wedding followed by a flood of baby pictures.

"This is Jill," Shay said with a laugh as she pointed at a baby with food all over her face.

"Yeah, but this is the one I really wanted you to see." Anne took a photo from the wall and handed it to Shay. Jill's long dark hair was piled on top of her head. She wore a light blue shimmering dress with white patent leather low-heeled shoes. Her face was made up, she wore lipstick and in her arms was a trophy. "That was taken after the pageant, and it was the last time anyone ever saw Jill dressed like that again. She was beautiful that day, but I'll admit to you in private that she's much more lovely being exactly who she is. That's yours, you can keep it."

"Oh, Anne, I can't take this from you."

Anne waved a hand dismissively. "I have plenty more." She patted an empty spot on the wall surrounded by Seth's and Will's pictures when they got married. There were plenty of Jude and Ricky too. "This spot is reserved for Jill and her love, and I know you're gonna be in those pictures, too."

"I put sunscreen on my face before I came over here, and now I've teared up, and it's in my eyes," Shay said with a sniff.

202

Anne grabbed her by the hand. "Come on, you blubbering fool, I've got some eyedrops in the bathroom."

"In your face, wanker," Jill yelled just before she did a cannonball next to Jude in the pool.

Ella smiled as she watched the horseplay. "Jill's gaining weight, which means she's happy."

"Yeah, she's being fed at home," Vivian said as she, Ella, Anne, and Chloe enjoyed the shade beneath the patio while the rest of the Savoy family played in the water.

Anne watched all the commotion from behind a very large pair of sunglasses that made her look like a bug. "Shay's still thin, you reckon she's happy?" she added with a smirk.

They watched as Shay sneaked up behind Jill and dunked her. For a moment, she laughed, then yelped just before being dragged beneath the surface. Chloe smiled and said, "She's ecstatic."

"The trip and the fall happened very quickly," Vivian noted with concern. "That's the only thing that troubles me."

Ella reached across the table and squeezed Vivian's hand. "Well, you can stop worrying about that. Someone once told me time doesn't have a lot to do with it, when it's right, it's right."

Anne shook her head. "That's not how I said it."

"I wasn't talking about you." Ella jutted her chin. "I heard it from someone brilliant."

"It was me, Ella. I told you that on the trip when *you* were worried."

Ella smacked her lips. "I just don't remember it that way," she said and smiled. "I'm certain it was someone brilliant."

"Do I have to?" Jill whined as Shay dragged her from the pool.

"Yes, I see skin cancer all day at work, now dry off," Shay said as they walked over to the table and she picked up a tube of sunscreen.

"I put that shit on before I got into the pool," Jill complained. "I'm still greasy."

"So you're gonna put it on again." Shay handed her a towel. "Dry off like I told you."

"That's right, Shay, you tell her," Vivian chided. "Make her mind you."

Jill glared at her. "Oh right, Mom, just—you rubbed that into my mouth, Shay." Jill wiped her tongue on her towel.

Shay glanced at everyone gathered around the table with a grin. "Quickest way to shut her up."

Anne threw back her head and laughed. "Hot damn, she learns so fast."

"Don't distract her, she's about to rub my butt," Jill said with a grin.

Shay handed Jill the tube of sunscreen. "That you can do yourself."

"The honeymoon is over, Jill," Vivian teased.

"That's right, Shay, don't spoil her now," Ella chimed in.

Shay tossed her towel at them. "Well, y'all can hush."

"They picking on you, sis?" Jude walked over and smacked Jill on the butt. "Is it because you finally have an ass now?"

Shay gave him a playful shove. "Don't damage that, it's taken a lot of cooking to build it."

"You gonna rag me too, honey?" Jill said and gazed at Shay pitifully.

Shay smiled and gave her a quick kiss. "Just because I love you."

The show of affection caused a round of "awws" from the group, and Jill ignored them as she wrapped her arms around Shay and said, "I love you too."

Epilogue

One year and two months later

"Anne, sit down, and, Ella, stop tattling," Shay snapped as she looked over her shoulder at the two.

"Tune 'em up, baby," Jill said with a smile as she merged Sally onto the interstate.

"I don't have to take orders from a monkey," Anne said haughtily.

Shay jutted her chin. "I gotcha, monkey. Sit down."

Ella threw back her head and laughed. "Oh, it feels so wonderful to be back on the road!"

Jill held up a finger. "I am not hunting fake Bigfoot this time."

"That's all right, y'all aren't getting the big bed in the back, either," Anne retorted.

"Shay, do people really get pleasure out of nipple clamps?"

"I've never used them, Ella, I really couldn't say," Shay said with a smile.

Jill glanced from the road. "Do not encourage them."

Shay looked over her shoulder. "But I highly recommend the vibrating dildo."

Shay laughed as Jill fussed. Anne took the seat beside Ella and said, "I told you we'd make another trip, now you have to say I'm right."

Ella shook her head and smiled. "That's not how I remember it."

"We may not juke and jive like we used to, Ella, but we've still got a lot of life left in us."

"That we do." Ella wrapped her arms around one of Anne's. "Last year, we made a match. This year, we need to make a baby."

Anne exhaled loudly. "Great, another harebrained scheme."

Ella smiled as she gazed at the gold band on Shay's finger as she reached out to stroke Jill's hair. "I want to thank you both for bringing us on your honeymoon."

Jill glanced up in the mirror and smiled. "We couldn't think of a better way to spend it."

About the Author

Robin Alexander is the author of the Goldie Award-winning *Gloria's Secret* and many other novels for Intaglio Publications, including *Gloria's Inn, Gift of Time, The Taking of Eden, Love's Someday, Pitifully Ugly, Undeniable, A Devil in Disguise, Half to Death, Gloria's Legacy, A Kiss Doesn't Lie, The Secret of St. Claire, Magnetic, The Lure of White Oak Lake, The Summer of Our Discontent, Just Jorie, Scaredy Cat, The Magic of White Oak Lake, Always Alex, The Fall, Ticket 1207* and *Next Time*.

She was also a 2013 winner of the Alice B Readers Appreciation Award, which she considers a true feather in her cap.

Robin spends her days working with the staff of Intaglio and her nights with her own writings. She still manages to find time to spend with her partner, Becky, and their three dogs and four cats.

You can reach her at robinalex65@yahoo.com. You can visit her website at www.robinalexanderbooks.com and find her on Facebook.

Made in the USA
San Bernardino, CA
08 November 2017